Lucky Break

ACCIDENT!

Nikki Fisher

First published in Great Britain in 1995.
Text copyright © 1995 Nikki Fisher.
The moral right of the author has been asserted.

Bloomsbury Publishing PLC, 2 Soho Square, London W1V 6HB.
A CIP catalogue record for this book is available from The British Library
ISBN 0 7475 2149 2
Cover design by Alison Withey.
Cover illustration by Paul Kidby.
Text design by AB3.
Printed and bound in Great Britain by
Cox & Wyman Ltd, Reading, Berkshire.

1

As THE OPEN-TOPPED sports car zipped through Whiston's main streets, Ollie's long, blonde hair streamed out behind her. Her honey-coloured complexion had been polished by the chill air until her cheeks almost matched the car's red paintwork.

Will, the MG's proud owner, concentrated on skilfully navigating his way through the tail-end of the morning rush hour.

The limited space behind their two seats was crammed with bulging carrier bags. Lashed to the boot rack was a brass-bound cabin trunk, so large it dwarfed the car.

A smile of pleasure played around Ollie's lips as she relished the prospect which lay ahead of her. She was on the brink of achieving an ambition which she'd been working towards ever since her teens.

Mrs Connolly, a determined, middle-aged woman urged her teenage daughter through the throng of pedestrians. 'Come along, Janine, or you'll be so late for class you'll miss warm-up.'

'Mum, I'm not a kid any more!' Janine protested. 'I can find my own way to college. You don't need to come with me every day. She looked at her mother with large brown eyes that looked even larger because of the way her dark chestnut hair was severely shaped back into a tight bun. Anyway, I don't care if I am late!' she said, stubbornly shrugging off her mother's grip and pausing to catch her breath.

'I really don't know how you expect to get anywhere in ballet with that sort of attitude!' her mother snapped.

'Mum, the way I feel at the moment,' Janine said, shifting the heavy bag to the other shoulder, 'I don't suppose I'll make it to the end of the road.'

'Didn't I warn you not to stay up watching that film?' her mother scolded. 'You can't afford to have late nights.'

'Mum! Like Dad says, I am entitled to relax sometimes,' Janine protested.

Mrs Connolly pursed her lips. 'Your father's trouble is he doesn't realise the amount of dedication being a dancer takes. He's too soft and you can wrap him round your little finger.'

'Anyway,' Janine said moodily, 'I still got to bed by half past nine.'

'Exactly,' her mother agreed, taking the bag from her, 'and just look at the state of you this morning – fit for nothing!'

'I just wish it wasn't so cold,' Janine complained.

'Cold?' Her mother sounded surprised. 'But it's a lovely day.'

Ollie suddenly cried out. 'Left here, Will.'

Ignoring the hoots of protest from startled drivers, Will swung the wheel and they swept in through the main gates of Whiston City General Hospital.

'The Accident and Emergency Unit's at the top of the drive,' Ollie pointed, 'by those ambulances.'

Disregarding the yellow lines and no parking signs, Will cruised to a halt as Dean, the overweight porter, ambled through the double doors, scratching his non-designer stubble.

'Oi!' he shouted, 'you can't park there. Can't you read? This is for emergency vehicles only.'

Ollie, without bothering to open the door, vaulted athletically out of the car. She gave

Dean a glowing smile. 'But this is an emergency,' she said sweetly. 'Do you have a wheelchair?'

Taken aback, Dean blinked. 'What? Oh, yes, sure,' he said, dutifully going back inside.

'Will,' Ollie said, blowing him a kiss, 'thanks so much for bringing me.'

He beamed. 'Always a pleasure to see you, Ollie.'

A frown appeared across her forehead. 'I'm sorry about the delay. I hope it hasn't thrown your schedule?'

'No problem,' Will said, waving it aside. 'And for what it's worth, I thought you were fantastic this morning.'

Ollie, blushing under his compliment, wove the long, slender fingers of both hands through the handles of the carrier bags, plucking them from the car as Dean emerged with the wheelchair.

'Who needs this then?' he demanded.

'I do,' Ollie assured him.

'I thought you said this was an emergency?'

'Oh, but it is!' she assured him. 'I'm terribly late. Could you possibly help Will put my trunk on the wheelchair?'

Dean's jaw dropped. Ollie had swept past

him, through the double-doors, and was already marching up the corridor.

The Accident and Emergency Unit was busy, but when Ollie walked in she found her path blocked by the white-uniformed bulk of Sister Broadhurst.

Middle-aged and unmarried, Margery Broadhurst was a dedicated career nurse with years of experience in dealing with wayward patients – or staff. Through her steel-rimmed glasses, she gave Ollie an icy glare and firmly announced, 'Members of the public not brought in by paramedics must use the main entrance and check in at reception.'

Ollie smiled. 'Yes, but I'm not the public.'

Margery Broadhurst raised an eyebrow. 'No?'

'Staff Nurse Olivia Bourne-Smith.'

'You are Nurse Smith?' The wild-looking girl standing before her was not Sister Broadhurst's idea of potential nursing material. But then, the choice of Nurse Smith for the unit had not been hers, it had been inflicted on her from above.

'Yes, Nurse Smith reporting for duty,' Ollie said with a grin, jokingly clicking her heels in exaggerated salute.

Unfortunately the movement proved too

violent for one of her bulging carrier bags. Its bottom burst, releasing a cascade of paperback novels, underwear and a big, brass alarm clock, which hit the green-and-grey polished tiles with a loud clatter.

Several members of staff who happened to be passing turned and smiled sympathetically, but Sister Broadhurst stooped and picked up the offending alarm clock. 'Perhaps, Nurse Smith,' she said, handing Ollie the clock, 'if you had actually used this, you might have managed to arrive on time for the first shift of your new job.'

Crawling round the floor, trying to recover her belongings and stuff them into other bags, Ollie managed to suppress a strong desire to laugh. Ever since childhood, her ability to see the ludicrous side of life had often bubbled up at inconvenient moments and got her into serious trouble with everyone from teachers onwards. 'Sorry, there was a slight problem during my journey here.'

But Ollie's explanation was interrupted as the transparent plastic doors burst open to admit Dean, pushing the wheelchair with Ollie's trunk balanced across its arms. 'So,' he asked loudly, 'where would you like this then?'

Sister Broadhurst couldn't believe what she saw. 'What exactly is it?' she asked grimly.

'This lady's trunk,' Dean explained.

As Margery Broadhurst took a deep breath, Ollie cut in quickly. 'This being my first day, I hoped you wouldn't mind if I left my luggage here while I pop out to look for somewhere to live.'

Sister Broadhurst gave Ollie an even sterner glare. The type of young girls she was expected to deal with these days! 'It's kind of you to ask, but since you have, I do mind. What's more, Nurse Smith, unless you're in uniform and ready for duty in under fifteen minutes, you won't need anywhere to live. You'll be on the next train out!' Margery Broadhurst turned and marched off between the lines of green curtained cubicles, pausing briefly to hurl one final remark over her shoulder. 'And do something about your dreadful hair!'

'I suppose I could always shave my head,' Ollie muttered cheerfully to herself. 'Probably go nicely with the sackcloth and ashes you'll be expecting me to wear.'

An attractive nurse in her early thirties, with large blue eyes, auburn hair and wearing a navy blue uniform, broke away from the small group which had been enjoying the cabaret. As she got closer, Ollie couldn't help noticing how tired the nurse looked, but she still gave Ollie a brief smile and her voice was cheerful enough. 'Hi, I'm Senior Staff Nurse Barbara Heywood, known as Ba for short.'

'Hi, I'm Staff Nurse Olivia Smith,' Ollie said ruefully. 'I'm afraid I haven't made a very good first impression with Sister.'

'Well, you certainly didn't manage to slip in unnoticed,' Ba admitted. 'There are two things to remember about Sister Broadhurst. The first is, her bite is far worse then her bark.'

Ollie looked puzzled. 'Shouldn't that be the other way round?'

Ba shook her head. 'I'm afraid not! Secondly, but most important of all, Sister Broadhurst is not only the most professional and experienced nurse you're ever likely to meet, but she knows more about acute nursing than most people in this entire building.' Ba checked her fob watch. 'And she always sticks to her word. Which means you now have exactly twelve minutes left in this job unless you do as she says. Vee!' Ba called to a health-care assistant. 'Would you show Nurse Smith where the staff locker room is, so that she can stash her stuff and get changed?'

'Sure,' Vee said. 'You certainly don't believe in travelling light. You look like a Christmas tree with all those carrier bags hanging from you.'

Ollie shrugged. 'I can never decide what to leave behind,' she admitted.

'Well, I'll wheel the coffin out for you,' Vee said, taking control of the wheelchair. 'By the way, I heard you telling old Broadsides you needed somewhere to stay. If you're stuck, there's plenty of room at my place.'

Before Ollie had a chance to answer, a male voice interrupted. 'Excuse me, Nurse, I'm sure these couldn't possibly belong to anyone around here but you.'

Ollie turned to find a white-coated young man with flashing eyes and dark, short-cropped hair. He was holding up a pair of minuscule royal-blue pants which she must have dropped but, in all the fuss, failed to recover.

'Hello,' he continued, silkily introducing himself, 'I'm Tarquin Royston, Senior House Officer in this madhouse.' He paused to display a smile which showed off the contrast between his perfect white teeth and his skiing tan. 'And I certainly look forward to working very closely with someone who wears anything like these.'

'Oh, well,' Ollie said, without a hint of a smile, 'if you're that keen on them, Doctor, why don't you keep them?'

Vee, managing to smother a loud snort, swiftly led Ollie away.

Staff Nurse Jill Thomson, a neat girl with short, black hair and earnest brown eyes, who like Ollie had only recently qualified and joined the unit full time, had overheard Tarquin and Ollie's exchange. Jill took a step towards the doctor, but Tarquin, having failed to impress Ollie and been made to look foolish in the process, hastily stuffed the pants into the pocket of his white coat, brushed past Jill and stalked off scowling.

Janine was standing at the foot of a flight of stone steps which led up to the imposing front doors of the Dance Academy. They had never looked so steep.

'I'm just going round to Dance Rhythms,' Mrs Connolly said. 'I'm going to have to change your new leotard. It must have been wrongly marked. It's far too big for you.'

'OK, Mum.'

'But I'll be back in plenty of time for lunch.'

Janine pulled a face. 'I'm not sure I'll bother

today, Mum. I don't feel very hungry.'

'Nonsense, dear,' her mother said brightly. 'Don't forget what Madame said. Two of the keys to building stamina, apart from exercise, are plenty of rest and a healthy diet.'

'Yes, Mum,' Janine said meekly, but without enthusiasm.

'Well,' her mother said, flapping her daughter away with her hands, 'off you go, or you'll miss warm-up altogether.'

As she walked off, Janine dutifully made her way up the steps. She had almost reached the top when her left leg suddenly seemed to go from under her. For an instant, the girl hung poised in mid air. Then, with a loud scream, she fell backwards, bumped and rolled down the stone steps, before landing heavily on the pavement. Her bag and one leg were tucked awkwardly beneath her. Her hair had come out of the tight bun and spilled out across the paving stones.

Hearing the scream, her mother rushed back and crouched down beside her daughter. 'Janine! What happened? Are you all right?'

Several passers-by stopped and a secretary popped her head round the Academy's front door to see what the fuss was about.

'It's my right leg,' Janine said, her face screwed up with pain. 'I can't move it.'

'Ring for an ambulance,' her mother called to the secretary, who immediately rushed inside.

Janine protested. 'Mum! Don't make such a fuss.'

'Nonsense, you may have broken something,' her mother insisted. She turned to a woman bystander and explained confidentially, 'You see, my daughter's a ballerina.'

Janine, too embarrassed to listen and in considerable pain, turned her head away.

2

ON THE OUTSKIRTS of the city, in the paramedics' duty room of Whiston Ambulance Station, Colin was just about to take a gulp of tea when the red emergency phone rang. 'Typical,' he grumbled, while his colleague, Karen, took the call and noted down the details. 'A twelve-hour shift, no breakfast and I've only got to look at a cup of tea to make that thing ring!'

'Never mind, Col,' Karen said as she shrugged on her green-and-yellow reflecting jacket and together they headed out towards their ambulance, 'think of the good it does your figure.'

Colin pretended to tuck his paunch in behind the wheel and started the engine. 'I'll have you know, I'm very fit for a man in my condition. What have we got?'

'Suspected fracture in the High Street.'

'Somebody tripped over their wallet?'

Karen shook her head. 'No more details, but it happened at the far end, outside the Dance Academy.'

The ambulance swung out of the yard into the traffic and Karen hit the emergency button, hoping the blaring siren and flashing blue lights would clear their path.

Having hastily put on her pale-blue uniform, Ollie returned to the Accident and Emergency Unit just as a woman, her left hand wrapped in a heavily bloodstained tea towel, was being shown into a vacant cubicle.

Dean was wheeling a young boy with a broken arm towards the Plaster Room. He paused to grumble at Ollie, 'Hospital porters aren't nurses' servants, you know.'

But before Ollie had a chance to reply, Sister Broadhurst's voice boomed down the corridor, 'Nurse Smith!'

Ollie scuttled obediently towards her. 'Sister?'

'There's no time for idle chatter in a busy A and E unit,' Sister Broadhurst snapped, before she caught sight of Ollie's hair, which was already threatening to escape from the swiftly inserted pins. 'I won't issue repeated warnings about your hair. I will not tolerate untidiness in any form.'

'Sorry, Sister,' Ollie mumbled through a

mouthful of pins as she fought to gain control of the stray locks. 'Sometimes it develops a life of its own.'

'Nurse Smith, your six-month contract means you are only here on probation. It's up to you to prove your worth.'

'Yes, Sister,' Ollie said. Having reached this moment after years of training, she really didn't want to mess things up.

'Usually,' Margery Broadhurst continued, 'I like to talk to the nurses arriving in the unit, introduce them to people and show them round, but your late arrival means there won't be time for that. You'll just have to pick things up as best you can. Maybe we'll have the opportunity of meeting first thing tomorrow. That is, if you are still with us and manage to arrive on time. For what's left of this morning, I suggest you join Senior Staff Nurse Heywood. She will be your preceptor, your main point of reference within the department.' Having checked the notes chalked up on the status board, Sister Broadhurst pointed along the avenue of cubicles. 'She's in cubicle four dealing with a burns case.'

'Just try and stay calm, Sarah,' Jill Thomson said to the distressed woman she was swiftly wheeling through from reception in a wheelchair. 'The doctor will soon take a look at you.'

'It's not me I'm worried about,' Sarah replied, stroking her stomach. 'It's my baby.'

'You really shouldn't have walked all the way here.'

'I was in town doing some shopping,' Sarah explained. 'But I've had this sore throat for a couple of days and while I was going round the supermarket, I started to feel all hot and peculiar. I honestly thought I was going to faint.'

'All the more reason for calling an ambulance,' Jill said, turning into cubicle ten.

'I don't like making a fuss,' Sarah said. 'Aidan, that's my husband, says I keep on imagining something's going to go wrong with the baby, but it's our first, you see. I'm nearly forty – we've been trying such a long time and I don't know what I'd do if …' The woman's voice broke off. She clasped a fist over her mouth, her face reddened and, although her eyes were tightly closed, tears rolled down her flushed cheeks.

'I'm sure everything's going to be fine,' Jill said, handing her some tissues. 'Let's get you undressed and on to the bed so we can have a proper look at you.'

* * *

Ollie found cubicle four where Ba Heywood was attending to Mrs Roberts, an old lady wearing only nightie and slippers.

As Ollie joined them, despite suffering from minor shock, or perhaps because of it, the old lady was chatting away to Ba, 'I was sitting in my chair, having a cup of tea. But I must have nodded off and my hand just dropped on to the guard of the electric fire.'

'Good thing it had a guard,' Nurse Heywood said. Using tweezers, she removed the antibacterial dressing put on by the paramedics and dropped it into the bowl Ollie held out. The joints at the base of the woman's fingers were swollen and inflamed. 'What's all this shiny stuff you've got on the wound, Mrs Roberts?'

'Best butter,' Mrs Roberts assured her proudly. 'Even during the war we only ever had butter. In them days, to make our ration go further, we used to melt it down, mix it with milk and then let it set again.'

Smiling, Ba Heywood shook her head. 'Yes, Mrs Roberts, but the only thing you should ever put on a burn is cold water to cool the wound down and restrict the damage. You should never use anything greasy.' Ba turned to

Ollie and said quietly, 'Bearing in mind Mrs Roberts' advanced age, as a matter of course, we'd better check for any heart problems.'

After taking the old lady's pulse, Ba fitted a Velcro cuff round the patient's upper arm and said to Ollie, 'When I've taken Mrs Roberts' blood pressure, you can clean the wound off so it's ready for the doctor to look at.'

Mrs Roberts asked suspiciously, 'Will it hurt?'

Ollie gave her a broad, comforting smile. 'The way I do it, Mrs Roberts,' Ollie assured her, 'you'll probably think you've been brushed by a butterfly's wing.'

'You nurses, I don't know how you do it,' the old lady babbled on. 'Me, I pass out at the first sight of blood. My Ernest used to love liver and onions, but I told him, if you want liver, you can cook it yourself!'

'It's her right leg,' Mrs Connoly said, fussing around Colin and Karen, who were busy immobilising both of Janine's legs with splints before lifting her on to the waiting trolley.

'They know that, Mum!' Janine hissed, through teeth already gritted against the pain. 'You've told them at least twenty times already!'

'Yes, but it's very important they understand,' her mother insisted. 'Janine's a dancer,' she said proudly to Karen.

Colin winked encouragingly at Janine, 'Don't worry, Mrs —?'

'Connolly.'

'Right, Mrs Connolly. There's no need to worry. We hardly ever take off the wrong leg.'

In spite of the pain Janine grinned, but her mother's hand flew up to her mouth in horror at Colin's horrifying suggestion.

Karen gave Colin a filthy look and said quietly, 'Ignore him, Mrs Connolly. My colleague's got a rather warped sense of humour.'

Mrs Connolly stroked Janine's head. 'I wish we'd been able to afford private health care for you.'

'If it'll make you feel any better,' Colin offered cheerfully, 'I could always charge you for the ride to the hospital.'

'Colin!' Karen hissed fiercely, as they prepared to lift Janine on to the trolley and into the ambulance.

'Let's have a look at the runners and riders,' Angus McFee, the Accident and Emergency consultant said to Tarquin and Margery

Broadhurst, as he glanced down the status board. He was a tall man with large hands, a mop of wavy, sandy hair and an easy manner. His bright blue eyes twinkled over half-glasses. 'Tarquin, why don't you look at the burns woman and then —'

Jill interrupted him just then. 'Mr McFee, I've got a woman I think you should see in ten. She's six months pregnant, with a high temperature and swollen glands. She's in some pain – she almost fainted while she was out shopping.'

'Prices in the shops are quite alarming,' Angus observed mildly in his faint Scottish accent.

But Jill, ignoring the consultant's light-hearted remark, added, 'She's an elderly prim.'

'A prima gravida, eh? In that case, Nurse Thomson, lead the way.'

Ollie had just finished cleaning the best butter off Mrs Roberts' hand when Tarquin, flanked by Margery Broadhurst, sailed into the cubicle to take a look at the wound. Having scowled at Ollie, Tarquin glanced briefly at Mrs Roberts' notes. Then, because she was old, he addressed her in a voice loud enough to be heard in reception. 'That's a nasty burn you've got there, Mrs Roberts.'

'It's my hand that's damaged, you know, Doctor,' Mrs Roberts scolded, 'not my hearing.'

Tarquin looked surprised. 'What? Oh, sorry,' he apologised, flushing slightly. 'How did you do this?'

'On an electric fire.'

'In that case, I'll just check your heart rate.'

Ollie interrupted, 'Staff already checked.'

'Thank you, Nurse,' he said heavily, 'but I'd like to see for myself.'

Tarquin reached into his pocket and pulled out his stethoscope without realising that, entangled in the ear pieces, were Ollie's royal-blue pants.

He was far too busy concentrating on Mrs Roberts' heartbeat to notice them fluttering to the floor. Nor did he see how surprised the old lady was to find a doctor producing ladies' underwear from his pocket like a conjurer.

Ollie struggled to suppress a fit of giggles, while Sister Broadhurst's eyebrows went into orbit.

Tarquin, totally unaware of the minor sensation he'd caused, took off his stethoscope. 'Your heart sounds fine. You just need a short course of antibiotics to clear up any possible infection, but you ought to leave the wound uncovered as much as possible so it can breathe.'

'Thank you, Doctor,' Mrs Roberts said cautiously, still unsure how to react to a man whose pockets contained items of lingerie.

Tarquin turned to Sister. 'What's next?'

'A cut hand in cubicle six.'

'Right,' he said, wondering why she wasn't moving.

Margery Broadhurst said loftily, 'I think, Mr Royston, you have just dropped something.' She sniffed her disapproval before leaving the cubicle.

Tarquin glanced down at the pants which he was beginning to think were sent to haunt him and scowled before he stalked off after her, muttering, 'Sister, there's a perfectly simple explanation…'

As his voice faded away and Ollie tactfully picked up the pants, Mrs Roberts said confidentially, 'What a strange young man.'

'You've a throat as red as the old Russian flag and the lymph nodes in your neck and armpits are very swollen,' Angus McFee told Sarah, 'but it may be nothing more than a nasty virus.'

'I'm so worried it'll affect the baby,' Sarah murmured.

'At the moment the baby's got a heartbeat strong enough for a scrum half,' Angus assured her, 'but we'll need to do some tests on you before we can be certain. We'll need blood and urine samples. When we get the results of those I'll come and take another look at you. In the meantime, just try to rest easy.'

Jill said, 'Sarah, as the results could take about an hour, would you like me to contact your husband, so he can be here with you?'

Sarah weakly shook her head. 'I wish you could, but Aidan's working away from home. He only comes back at weekends.'

Janine's stretcher was wheeled into the A and E unit, and Colin briskly reported to Ba, 'This is Janine, who's got a suspected fracture of the right tibia.'

The patient was wheeled away to a cubicle and Ba pointed Mrs Connolly towards reception.

Karen turned on Colin, 'You really must stop winding people up like that, Col!'

'Well!' Colin growled. 'If you ask me, that woman's definitely one pirouette short of a pas de deux.'

Karen smiled in spite of herself as she dug her elbow into Colin's ribs.

Jill, returning from delivering Sarah's samples, spotted Vee collecting a replacement roll of paper sheets from the clinical supply room and asked 'So, what have you heard about this new nurse?' She desperately tried to sound casual, but Jill knew another nurse on the unit was direct competition for her, in more ways than one.

As far as her job was concerned, at the end of their six-month contracts, it was quite likely there would be only one vacancy, if that. Jill hadn't felt very secure even before she discovered another nurse was coming. Now that Ollie had arrived, she suddenly had serious doubts about her future at Whiston City General.

The fact that she'd seen the way Tarquin Royston had eyed up the new girl only made matters worse.

Vee shrugged. 'Well, she calls herself Ollie. Broadsides calls her Nurse Smith, but I saw an old label on that trunk of hers which said Miss Olivia Bourne-Smith, if you please.'

'Where do you think she did her training?'

'According to my friend, Tina, in Personnel, it was one of the London hospitals,' Vee replied.

'Don't you think it's a bit odd she's got a

place here?' Jill said thoughtfully. 'I mean, I trained here, but these days it's almost impossible to get jobs away from the hospital where you do your training.'

'Well,' said Vee, lowering her voice, 'Tina hinted there was some sort of scandal and she had to leave.'

Jill looked wide-eyed at Vee. 'What sort of scandal?'

'Tina wouldn't say.' Vee was worried she might already have said too much. 'Hey, listen, you mustn't breath a word of this to anyone.'

'Of course I won't,' Jill said, but then she looked puzzled. 'But if she got chucked out of the London hospital—'

'I didn't say that,' Vee insisted.

'All right, but she still had to leave, which makes it even odder she got taken on here.'

'Maybe, with a name like Bourne-Smith, she knows the right kind of people to ask,' Vee suggested.

Jill couldn't avoid suffering a pang of envy when she thought of the tremendous struggle her parents had had to keep her on at school long enough to complete her education. They worked long hours, just about scraping a living from a little newsagent's shop in a northern town.

Jill had failed to get on a nurses' training course in her home town and was turned down by several other hospitals before eventually being accepted at Whiston. But having to live away from home had placed even more strain on the family budget. It really hurt to find someone like Ollie strolling in, and possibly ending up taking her job, just because she knew the right people.

'I suppose,' Jill said bitterly, 'those sorts of people always get on.'

'Well, she certainly seems posh enough,' Vee said. 'When I offered her a room in my place, I got the feeling she didn't think it'd be good enough for her. And she arrived with a ton of stuff.'

'Some of which she managed to drop in front of Mr Royston,' Jill said, her voice heavy with disapproval.

Vee laughed as she remembered Ollie's put-down. 'Yes, she certainly put Master Tarquin back in his box!'

'Poor man,' Jill said.

'Don't you fret over him, Nurse Thomson. Tarquin Royston is more than capable of looking after himself.'

'Oh, I know that,' Jill said, colouring slightly.

'Even so, she shouldn't have embarrassed him the way she did.'

Vee's eyes widened. 'Embarrass him? Our Tarquin's got the hide of a rhino. Besides, he was the one waving her pants around.'

'I bet she dropped them on purpose, just to attract his attention.'

'Could it be,' Vee asked, cocking her head on one side, 'that you've got a touch of the hots for Tarquin?'

Jill looked genuinely shocked. 'What a horrible thing to say!' She stomped off towards the door. 'I just think Nurse Smith ought to watch her manners, that's all.'

But as the door closed Vee said to herself, 'There goes another lamb to the slaughter and she doesn't know it yet her own self!'

3

JANINE HAD BEEN transferred to the bed in cubicle five, where she was being given the official greeting by Ba. 'Hello, Janine. I'm Senior Staff Nurse Heywood, your named nurse, responsible for your care. If you have any problems while you're here, then you should ask for me.'

Janine smiled. 'Thank you.'

'Nurse Smith is going to help me undress you.'

Meanwhile Mrs Connolly found the middle-aged receptionist, Maureen, facing a backlog of patients as she struggled to enter their details into the computer.

'Twenty years I've worked here,' Maureen complained, as she tapped the keys. The computer bleeped in pain and Maureen stared in disbelief at the result on the screen. 'Why did they have to change the wretched programme!'

'I'm sorry,' said a young man who was pressing a bloodstained pad to his head, 'but I need to see someone soon. I'm bleeding all over the place.'

Without even looking at him, Maureen continued, 'The only thing I understand about computers is why they call that blinking light the cursor. I never stop cursing it!'

'We use a computer in the garage where I work, maybe I could help,' the young man suggested, leaning right over the counter to get a better look.

Shocked, Maureen instantly snatched up a file and hid the screen from him. 'You aren't allowed to see what's on there; it's highly confidential!'

'But they're my details,' he pointed out, reasonably. 'You've only got on the screen what I've just told you.'

'That's hardly the point!'

'Look,' the boy said in desperation, 'have you tried pressing enter?'

'Yes, of course I have,' Maureen said indignantly. But then she looked more doubtful. 'I'm sure I did.'

'Well, do it again, just in case.'

'Don't be silly, it couldn't be anything that simple!' Maureen said, but did it anyway and was amazed when the computer immediately responded favourably. 'Good heavens!'

'It's often something quite simple like that,' the young man said cheerfully.

Maureen looked up and smiled. 'That's very kind of you.' Then she noticed the drops of blood which were plopping on her desk. 'Do you know you're bleeding?'

The man nodded, dropping more blood, and said patiently, 'Yes, that's why I came.'

'Yes, well, we'll try and get someone to see you shortly.'

'How long do you think it might be?'

'There's a sign right there,' Maureen said, proudly pointing to a display which said, Estimated Waiting Time is currently 20 minutes. 'Next!'

'Ambulance Control to Papa, X-ray, Golf.'

'I thought it was too quiet to be true,' Colin said, as he unhooked the microphone from the radio. 'Papa, X-ray, Golf.'

Control came back. 'Can you attend an RTA at the intersection of Beverley Drive and Watson Street?'

'On our way,' Colin replied, hitting the emergency lights and siren as Karen skilfully accelerated out of heavy traffic.

'Police and fire service are already in attendance,' Control continued. 'Driver trapped and at least two injured passengers.'

* * *

Mrs Connolly, having eventually managed to complete the formalities in spite of Maureen's problems, returned to cubicle five just as Ollie and Ba had finished undressing Janine.

Ollie was bending down, stowing away the plastic bag of Janine's belongings in the rack beneath the bed, when Tarquin burst through the curtains. He wasn't pleased to see Ollie's blonde head appear, but he ignored her and concentrated on Janine. 'So, young lady, what have you been up to?'

Before Janine could speak, Mrs Connolly answered for her. 'She was on her way to class, but she fell down the steps of the Academy.'

'Thank you Mrs — er,' he glanced at the notes, 'Mrs Connolly.' He turned again to Janine. 'Your right leg?'

But Mrs Connolly was ahead of him. 'I do hope it's going to be straightforward. You see, my daughter's a dancer.'

'Mum. They don't want to know all that!'

Mrs Connolly bridled. 'There's no need to take that tone with me. It's very important they realise it isn't just any old leg they're dealing with, but a dancer's.'

As Tarquin sighed testily through clenched

teeth, Ba took Mrs Connolly by the shoulders and gently, but firmly, propelled her through the curtains and out into the aisle. 'Mrs Connolly, I'm sure you've had a very trying morning. Nurse Smith will show you where you can get a cup of tea.'

'I'd much rather be present during the examination.'

'Apart from hospital staff, Doctor Royston prefers to be alone with his patients.'

'But I'm her mother.'

'Mrs Connolly, your daughter is sixteen years old,' Ba pointed out, 'and perfectly capable of speaking for herself. Nurse Smith!' Ollie appeared through the curtains. 'Would you please take Mrs Connolly to reception for a cup of tea?'

Mrs Connolly, still looking unhappy, reluctantly allowed herself to be ushered back out into the main reception area. 'I meant to ask the doctor if he thought Janine would need plastic surgery,' she said anxiously.

Ollie looked baffled. 'For her leg?'

'No,' Mrs Connolly said impatiently, 'for that dreadful wound on her face.'

Ollie had to think very hard even to remember the slight graze. 'I doubt if plastic surgery will be necessary. Now, why don't you have a seat,' Ollie suggested. 'Tea with milk and sugar?'

'I don't suppose they have Earl Grey?'

Ollie smiled. 'I somehow doubt it, Mrs Connolly. You see, it comes from a vending machine.'

'Oh.'

But when Ollie returned, Mrs Connolly clearly wouldn't have noticed what she was drinking. She ignored it, merely cradling the plastic cup in one hand while she talked, half to herself, half to Ollie. 'I could see my Janine was special from the day she was born. It was her feet even then. The way she pushed, long before she could walk.'

Ollie nodded. 'So your daughter's always wanted to be a dancer?'

'Oh, of course. Mind you, there were times, if she hadn't had me behind her,' Mrs Connolly said, 'when she might have given up, but I knew she had it in her to really go places.'

'Does she skate too?' Ollie asked casually. 'I know several dancers who are very good ice-skaters.'

'She wanted to,' Mrs Connolly admitted, 'but I said, stick to what you're best at. Besides, I was always afraid she might have a dreadful accident. And now look what's happened!'

Suddenly Mrs Connolly's face crumpled. Tears ran down her cheeks.

'You mustn't upset yourself.' Ollie gently touched her arm. 'I'm sure your daughter's going to be fine.'

'But she's just won a place at the Royal Ballet School,' Mrs Connolly went on. 'We're only waiting to hear about the grant. I don't know what'll happen now.'

'Well, like I say —'

'Why are they taking so long?'

'You drink your tea, Mrs Connolly,' Ollie suggested, 'and when the doctor's finished, I'll come and get you.'

Karen brought the ambulance to a halt alongside a policeman who was busy trying to persuade gawping drivers to go round two severely damaged cars. Firemen were working on one vehicle with cutting equipment.

Colin grabbed his bag and walked over to a second police officer. 'What have we got?' he asked.

'The people in the other car all seem to be OK apart from cuts and bruises, but the driver's trapped in this one. The passengers are over there on the pavement.'

'Karen,' Colin called out over the noise of the cutters, 'would you check out the passengers while I do the driver.'

Through the open driver's window, Colin could see a badly injured young girl. Her long hair was matted with blood which also streamed down her face from an injury on her forehead. Her eyes were closed.

Noticing that the rear passenger door immediately behind the driver was only slightly damaged, Colin asked the fire officer, 'OK if I climb in behind her?'

Receiving a curt nod, Colin quickly clambered inside, put on rubber gloves and felt round her, checking for vital signs of life. He found a feeble pulse but she had almost stopped breathing. Although it was awkward working from behind the patient, Colin managed to establish an airway by poking a tube into her mouth and down her throat. Then, using a mask and bag, he started to pump oxygen into her from a portable cylinder. After he'd pumped the bag three times he checked the pulse again. It was still very weak. She was clearly suffering from loss of fluids due to internal injuries.

Above the noise of the cutter, he called to the fire officer, 'How much longer?'

The fireman held up all five fingers and shrugged.

'She can't wait that long,' Colin muttered to himself. 'I'll just have to do the best I can from here.'

Starting to reach round the girl's seat, Colin eventually found a vein in her arm, inserted the Venflon needle, taped it down, and then, through its butterfly-shaped opening, gave her one unit of haemacell.

Ollie met Ba leaving Janine's cubicle. 'What's the news?'

'It is a fracture,' Ba confirmed. 'We won't know any more until she's been to X-ray, but it shouldn't be a problem. Would you clean up the minor abrasions on her arms and face?'

Ollie leaned towards Ba and said quietly. 'I couldn't help noticing when we were undressing Janine that she's terribly thin.'

'Yes,' Ba admitted. 'I suppose she is a bit but, as her mother never stops saying, she is a dancer. I'd probably be more like a fairy queen than a fairy elephant if I danced all day long, seven days a week.'

'I know they have a pretty rigorous schedule,' Ollie agreed, 'but I still think Janine looks underweight for her age and height.'

'Maybe,' Ba said, thoughtfully. 'Why don't you have a chat with Janine while you're cleaning her up and she's waiting to go up to X-ray? See what you can find out – but don't spend too much time on it,' Ba warned. 'Remember there are other patients needing attention.'

'Must keep up the cost-effective flow of the department, I suppose,' Ollie commented.

'You know perfectly well that isn't what I mean,' Ba admonished. 'It's a question of where we're most needed and if Janine isn't seeking help, we can't force it on her.'

Karen had calmed down two of the young men who had been passengers in the crashed car. Although covered in blood, one was suffering from nothing worse than superficial cuts. The other also had a nasty gash in his leg, caused by being hurled against the parcel shelf, and possible whiplash. Once she'd fitted him with a cervical collar she went to see how Colin was doing.

There was a violent squeal of rending metal as the roof of the car was peeled back like a tin of sardines being opened.

'Phew, that's better,' Colin sighed with relief, sweating from the exertions of trying to revive the girl in such a restricted space. 'How are the others?'

'Fine. One's on the trolley with a collar on and the other bloke's sitting in the ambulance with a blanket round him complaining he hadn't even finished paying for the suit he's ruined. What can I do?'

'Now you can get to her face, can you use the bag and mask while they release her legs?'

'Have you always been a dancer?' Ollie asked, as she needlessly busied herself tidying equipment on the trolley at the head of Janine's bed.

'I wasn't actually born doing arabesques,' Janine said sulkily, 'if that's what you mean.'

Ollie ignored the girl's tone. 'Any more than I was born clutching a thermometer and a bed-pan. But then, I didn't decide to take up nursing until just before I left school.'

The moment Janine felt she was no longer the focus of attention she noticeably lightened up. 'So why did you?'

'Do you want the glib answer or an honest one?'

'The real reason,' Janine said, sounding genuinely interested.

'I had an elder brother, Edward, who I absolutely worshipped.' Ollie folded a white towel as she spoke. 'Do you have any brothers or sisters?'

'No, I'm an only child.'

'So am I now,' Ollie said sadly. 'But when I was little, Edward and I did everything together. I thought he was the most wonderful person in the entire universe. But just before his twenty-first, he had a routine blood test.' As she remembered, Ollie stood still, the towel wrapped over one arm, gazing into the distance, reliving that moment. 'When the results finally came through, we didn't believe them. They said he had abnormalities in the blood. Then they carried out a whole lot more tests and it turned out Edward had a form of leukaemia which normally only affects older people, and that it was in a very advanced stage.'

'How awful!' Janine said quietly.

Ollie smiled wistfully. 'The most memorable present Edward got for his twenty-first birthday was his first dose of chemotherapy. They also stuffed him with antibiotics and immunoglobulin injections, but it was all much too late. The disease had progressed too far before being diagnosed. In a few months I watched Edward change from a strong, handsome man to a frail, helpless invalid.'

'That would have been enough to put me off nursing for life,' Janine said.

'If I hadn't loved him so much, it might have had the same effect on me too,' Ollie admitted. 'But I felt so useless. I desperately wanted to help him. I'd have done anything to ease his suffering, but I didn't know how. I decided to take up nursing so that I'd never be in that position again. My mother's reaction was the exact opposite. She absolutely refused to visit Edward in hospital. Daddy and I went all the time, but she never went once.'

'How awful!'

'When they decided there was nothing more they could do, Edward came home. No expense was spared. Mummy had a room set up specially and she hired a live-in nurse to look after him twenty-four hours a day. But she wouldn't set foot in that room herself. Eventually she packed him off into a hospice. Of course, they were wonderful to him, but it wasn't the same and Edward never did understand why his own mother wouldn't visit him. It was almost as if she was punishing him for getting sick, and he was terribly hurt.'

'Mothers!' Janine said bitterly.

'Oh, I understand her reaction,' Ollie said. 'I didn't agree with it and I got very angry with her, but the fact was, she simply could not face up to the truth. Her only beloved son was dying. She just refused to acknowledge it and as long as she didn't see the evidence, she could keep on ignoring it. Somehow she convinced herself that all his treatments and stays in hospital were rather like visits abroad. She kept telling herself that one day Edward would come back, miraculously the same as he'd left. But of course that wasn't true.'

'My mother doesn't listen either,' Janine said. 'She made her mind up years ago I should be a ballet dancer, and nothing's going to change it now.'

'Mine's never forgiven me for taking up nursing.'

'I would have thought she'd have been pleased after what happened to your brother.'

'No way! The minute I suggested it,' Ollie said, remembering the furious row which had blown up, 'she packed me off to a Swiss finishing school, thinking I'd grow out of it. You see, what Mummy had in mind for me was that I should become a proper little homemaker, marry well and restore the family's flagging fortunes. Unfortunately, I had other ideas.'

'I've tried to explain to Mum hundreds of times how I feel,' Janine said.

'About dancing?'

'It isn't that I don't like dancing. I do. It's just that sometimes it seems to have taken over my entire life.'

'There was a time when I was little,' Ollie said quietly, 'when I thought being a dancer would be the most wonderful thing. But unfortunately I'm too big in all the wrong places.'

'Me too,' Janine said. 'I'm so fat!'

Ollie couldn't help glancing at Janine's skinny wrists, but she kept talking. 'I suppose you have to keep to a very strict diet?'

'Oh, all the time. I've only got to look at something like an ice-cream to put on inches round my waist.'

'Do you know,' Ollie said thoughtfully, 'there's one thing I've always wondered about dancers.'

'What's that?'

'If you've got a big performance coming up and it happens to coincide with your period, how do dancers cope, especially if they suffer from bad period pains?'

Suddenly Janine looked away. 'That's not a problem. You just regulate it when you take the pill.'

'Is that what you do?'

Janine's face suddenly closed down completely. 'Look, my leg's hurting and I'm tired. Could you just leave me alone, please?'

'Sorry, yes, of course,' Ollie said. 'But I'll be back shortly to clean up those scratches on your face and arm.'

As Ollie walked towards her, Senior Staff Nurse Heywood glanced up from the forms she was completing. 'Any luck?'

'Janine's not very forthcoming,' Ollie said, 'but she definitely believes she's fat and I think she's stopped having periods.'

'Oh dear!' Ba said thoughtfully. 'By no means conclusive symptoms, but they certainly do ring alarm bells.'

4

MARGERY BROADHURST replaced the phone and turned to Ba. 'Ambulance control say there's an RTA on its way.'

'How many?'

'The driver of one of the vehicles has got severe leg, chest and head injuries and both her passengers have slight injuries. There's a second vehicle involved, but we don't know anything about that one. Send someone out to reception and warn them there are going to be delays. Nurse Thomson!'

'Yes, Sister?'

'I'm going to prepare Crash for an RTA. Would you find Mr McFee and Doctor Royston?'

Ollie could feel the atmosphere in the already busy Accident and Emergency Unit tightening by several notches. But while all the other staff calmly moved into gear, automatically seeming to know what was expected of them, Ollie, being new, wasn't sure of her role.

Ba came to her rescue. 'Ollie,' she said, 'you

could warn reception about the delays.'

'How long?'

Ba thought briefly. 'About an hour, I'd say.'

Lights flashing, siren blaring, Karen was heading for Whiston City General.

In the back of the gently swaying ambulance Colin was bending over the injured girl who was strapped into the trolley. She had an oxygen mask over her mouth and nose, and her legs were held by splints. 'Can you keep it steady for a while?' he asked Karen.

'You're OK for a bit right now.'

Colin carefully inserted a needle into the girl's arm, so he could set up the intravenous drip to help replace some of the fluids she had lost.

'Roundabout coming up!' Karen warned him.

'Don't worry, it's in.' But suddenly the ambulance lurched as Karen hit the brakes. Colin grabbed the side to stop himself being hurled forward. 'What was that?'

'An idiot who couldn't be bothered to check his mirror. He just pulled out in front of me,' Karen told him. 'How's she doing?'

'There's still a pulse,' Colin replied, 'but time's not on her side.'

'We should be there in under a minute if I can get round this next set of lights.'

In reception Ollie tried again to attract Maureen's attention. 'Excuse me,' she said firmly.

Without looking away from the screen, Maureen snapped back, 'Just a minute, please. Can't you see I'm busy?'

'We're quite busy back there too,' Ollie said pleasantly.

Maureen glanced up. 'Oh, I'm sorry, I thought you were another patient. You're a new face.'

Ollie smiled. 'Yes, I started today. I'm Nurse Smith. Call me Ollie.'

'Nice to meet you. I'm Bewildered of Whiston General. I'm trying to put a half-nelson on this computer thing, but it keeps fighting back. Maureen's the name. What's Ollie short for?'

'Olivia.'

Maureen's face suddenly lit up and she whooped, 'Ah, so you're the one!'

Ollie couldn't help wondering if this was the effect the almost legendary strain of continually working in Accident and Emergency had on people? The woman was certainly weird and possibly mad. 'I'm sorry?'

'I've been getting phone calls and taking messages for an Olivia all morning,' Maureen explained, 'and as nobody ever tells me anything around here, I didn't know who they were for.'

'Oh dear.'

Maureen picked up a sheaf of notes and handed them to Ollie. 'From Gavin, Martin, Colin, Robert, Alexander and Michael,' she reeled off.

'I'm really sorry about this.'

Maureen dismissed Ollie's apologies with a wave of the hand. 'Oh, please, don't feel bad. For a while, in between cut fingers and broken ankles, it quite brightened life up and they were all such nice sounding young men too, but it is becoming a bit time-consuming.'

'Please don't bother to take any more messages, Maureen. I'll call them all as soon as I get a chance and tell them to stop ringing me here.'

'Oh, there is just one more, from a girl called Hattie. Is that right?'

'Yes, my ex-flatmate.'

'That explains it. She said, would I tell you that walking out on her was one thing, but where the hell is the tin-opener?'

Ollie smiled. 'She's hopeless!'

'Well, now we've got that out of the way,' Maureen said with an enquiring smile, 'what was it you wanted?'

'Oh, yes. There are going to be delays for a while, there's a road traffic accident coming in.'

'Ah,' Maureen said with a smile. 'A piece of technology even I can cope with.' She stood up and dropped a one-hour delay card into the Estimated Waiting Time display and ignored the discontented shuffles of the waiting patients. 'Did Ba say how Simon was today?'

Ollie looked blank. 'Who's Simon?'

'Her little boy.'

'I didn't even know she was married.'

Maureen lowered her voice and whispered, 'Oh, she isn't married. It's a shame really. Daniel was a very nice young man.'

Ollie felt she was once more in danger of getting lost in Maureen's convoluted mind. 'Daniel?'

'He was the consultant here before Angus. Daniel and Ba made a lovely couple.'

'So what went wrong? Did he take fright when Simon came along?' Ollie asked and then added, with feeling, 'Typical man!'

'Oh, no, it was nothing like that,' Maureen shook her head. 'He'd asked her to marry him long before, but Ba kept turning him down. She said he wasn't grown-up enough yet to settle down. Poor Daniel. He comes to see Simon quite regularly, but the little boy's been poorly this last couple of days and I know Ba's been worried about leaving him.'

'I'll ask how he is when I get the chance,' Ollie said.

Jill found Mr McFee standing at the end of the unit peeping out through the slats of the Venetian blind. 'Did you know what a nice day it is out there in the big wide world?' he said.

Jill smiled and shook her head. 'I hate to ruin it for you, but Sister sent me to say there's an RTA on its way and she's gone to get Resus ready.'

Angus let out a long sigh and started to shamble up the corridor. 'And there was I thinking I might take a stroll in the sunshine.'

'Do you happen to know where Doctor Royston's gone?'

'He's been on all night and he's asleep on his feet,' Angus called back over his shoulder. 'I said he should kip down in the first empty office he found.'

As she was passing, Jill popped her head into cubicle ten.

Sarah, who'd been dozing, instantly opened her eyes. 'Have the results come back?'

'No, they'll be a while yet. Just relax.'

'I shan't be able to until I know everything's going to be all right.'

'I know it isn't easy,' Jill said, 'but try and think about something else to take your mind off it.'

'I did that just now,' Sarah admitted, 'and remembered I'd left the tins of cat food I need at the check-out.'

'I'll be back as soon as I can,' Jill said, already halfway through the curtains, 'but we've got an emergency coming in and I must go now.'

Ollie was about to return to the unit when Mrs Connolly cornered her. 'I've been sitting here for ages. Can you tell me what's going on?'

'The doctor's fairly certain your daughter has a simple fracture, but he'll have to see the X-rays first. She's waiting to go up there now, but I'm afraid there's going to be a bit of a delay.'

Mrs Connolly looked upset. 'What sort of delay?'

Ollie explained, 'We've got several patients

from a road traffic accident coming in any moment.'

'That seems hardly fair,' Mrs Connolly said. 'After all we were here first.'

Ollie bit back a rather hasty reply and instead said firmly, 'It's really a question of priorities. We have to decide which are the most urgent cases.'

'And my daughter isn't important? Very nice!'

Ollie sat beside Mrs Connolly. 'That isn't what I said, Mrs Connolly, but when it's a difference between life and death and a broken leg, I think you can understand why we consider somebody with a broken leg who is reasonably comfortable can wait while we treat another patient with severe multiple injuries.'

Mrs Connolly drew herself up. 'Well, I don't think that's good enough. After all, my daughter's whole future could be at stake.'

Ollie sighed, and then added politely, 'If that's how you feel.'

'I should like to speak to somebody in authority.'

Ollie stood up. 'I'll find someone as soon as possible, Mrs Connolly.'

*　　*　　*

Jill eventually found Tarquin. He had fallen asleep in one of the interview rooms, his feet on the coffee table and his head slumped down on to his chest.

She couldn't help thinking how vulnerable he looked, fast asleep like that, just like a little boy. She also remembered the crude expression Vee had used about her having 'a touch of the hots' for Tarquin!

Of course, Jill told herself, nothing could have been further from her true feelings. It was just that she admired his coolness and skill as a doctor, that was all. He was certainly very knowledgeable and always seemed willing to share that with the nurses, including Jill. She'd often seen him having private conversations, even with nurses from other departments, who all seemed eager to learn from his wisdom and experience.

But, as far as Jill was concerned, there really wasn't anything more to it than that. Was there?

'Doctor Royston,' she said gently, but he didn't stir.

She said it again, louder this time. It still had no effect and, having checked to make sure there was nobody out in the corridor, for the very first time Jill allowed herself the thrill of saying his first name out loud. 'Tarquin.' Just the sensation of the word passing her lips gave Jill a delicious thrill, though it had not the slightest effect on Tarquin himself.

Seeing that nothing else would work, Jill rather timidly shook his shoulder. As he stirred, she stepped back quickly but not before she caught a hint of his distinctive musky after-shave.

He rubbed his eyes and stiffly took his feet off the table. 'What's up?' he asked.

'There's an RTA due in any minute.'

'Right,' Tarquin yawned. He showed no sign of getting up but lolled lazily back in the chair, looking at Jill. 'Thanks for coming to get me.'

Jill felt herself starting to blush and cursed Vee for having put stupid ideas about Tarquin into her head. 'It was no trouble.'

'Of course, you could just have had me bleeped,' Tarquin said with a rather bleary version of one of his dazzling smiles, 'but you came personally.'

She was beginning to feel silly. 'I'd better go. Sister will be wondering where I am.'

'Sure, but just before you do . . .'

She was halfway out of the door and turned back to see what he wanted. 'Yes?'

'Remember the other day you were asking me about cases of spontaneous pneumothorax?' Jill nodded. 'Well, I've turned up some of my notes and I wondered if you'd like to see them?'

Jill smiled, happy to be back on firm professional ground. 'That's very kind of you.'

'The only thing is,' Tarquin added carefully, 'I foolishly left them in the car.'

'Oh, well, tomorrow would do.'

'Yes, of course,' Tarquin said casually, 'unless we happen to leave around the same time. I get let out tonight for good behaviour. Perhaps we could go down and get them out of the car this evening – together?'

Ollie reported back to Ba. 'I told Maureen about the hold-up and while I was out there she asked how Simon was today?'

A brief cloud passed across Ba's face. 'Oh, I expect he'll be all right.'

Ollie suddenly understood why Ba was looking tired. 'Were you up all night with him?'

'Well, yes and no. I slept in an armchair in his room, just in case he woke in the night. I'm sure it's nothing more than a snuffle, but I always feel a real heel dropping him off with the childminder when he's a bit off colour. But it's just the standard guilt feelings that go with the territory of being a working mum.' Ba gave a wry smile. 'Strange, isn't it? As nurses we're trained to deal perfectly calmly with the life-threatening situations of others on a daily basis. But when it comes to one of our own, we still fall apart at something as straightforward as a bit of a cold.'

'It's not the same, though, is it?' Ollie said. 'To survive the pressure, we're taught to keep a certain amount of emotional distance from the patients, but you can't do that with relatives, especially when they're little. The Mother Hen Syndrome. Speaking of which, Mrs Connolly nearly blew a gasket when I warned her Janine would have to wait a while for X-ray. She wants to speak to someone in authority.'

Ba's reply was interrupted by the arrival of porters and paramedics wheeling in a line of three stretchers.

'Coming through,' Colin said loudly. The victim on the first stretcher, which Colin and Karen were wheeling, was still unconscious. There was dark, drying blood in her hair. Karen was carrying the bag for the drip.

Ba waved them all through. 'Straight into Crash.'

Ollie asked, 'Do you want me in there too?'

As Ba fell into line behind the third stretcher, she called back over her shoulder, 'No, you stay and look after things here. Have you cleaned up Janine's cuts?'

'Not yet.'

'Do that first, then just keep an eye on the others out here. If there are any problems, you know where I am.'

Dean was leaving Crash when he met Jill Thomson heading in the opposite direction.

'Where's that new nurse?' Dean asked. 'Why isn't she in there?'

'I've no idea, Dean. That's up to Broadsides to decide.'

Being from a similar background, Dean often felt he had more in common with Jill than with some of the other members of staff and treated her as an ally. But it was a relationship Jill was trying to avoid. When they first met and Jill had been feeling a bit small and over-whelmed by her new surroundings, Dean had often put in a kind word, for which Jill had been grateful. Unfortunately Dean had taken her gratitude to mean rather more than she'd intended.

'Seems to me,' Dean continued, 'Nurse Smith thinks she's a bit above the rest of us.'

Even though that thought had already crossed Jill's mind, it wasn't something she wanted to pursue with Dean. Noncommittally she said, 'I wouldn't know.'

But Dean was still blocking her path. 'Look at the way she got me carrying her luggage for her, as if I was some sort of servant,' he grumbled. 'And she doesn't half talk posh. Seems a bit funny her being here at all, doesn't it? I mean, it's all competition for your job, isn't it? And things are tight enough as it is.' Dean scratched his head. 'How d'you reckon she got the job here in the first place?'

Jill couldn't stop herself passing on the gossip. 'I heard it was by pulling strings.'

'Yes,' Dean nodded, 'that sounds like her style, but it's not fair on you, is it?'

Though she knew she'd asked for it, Jill didn't want Dean's pity. 'I must get on.'

But before she could make her escape, Dean blocked her path. 'I don't suppose you could lend me a fiver, could you? Only, I'm starving and I came out without my wallet. I could pay you back tomorrow.'

Dean was infamous around the department,

for constantly trying to borrow money. They were debts he was slow to repay. He relied on the principle that most people didn't like to ask for their money back, so he usually avoided paying them back at all.

'Sorry, Dean,' Jill said, neatly sidestepping him, 'but I'm down to small change myself.'

'A pound for a burger would do,' he said hopefully, but Jill was gone before he could finish the sentence.

Ollie, wearing surgical gloves, was using gauze swabs and an antiseptic solution to clean off carefully the grazes on Janine's arm and face. 'I'm afraid you'll have to wait a while for X-ray. Everyone's a bit tied up with an emergency.'

'I'll be perfectly OK here,' Janine said.

'Is your leg comfortable?' Ollie asked.

Janine pulled a slight face. 'I'm fine, don't worry.'

'Would you like your mother to come through and keep you company?'

'Does she have to?'

'That's up to you. I'm afraid she isn't taking the news about the hold-up quite so calmly. I left her in a mood to ring her member of parliament, the newspapers or the Queen.'

'That's typical of my mother! She can be really embarrassing sometimes. If we go to buy something simple, like a pair of ballet flats, we've only to get inside the door and she's demanding to see the manager!'

'I know what you mean,' Ollie sympathised. 'I swear whenever my mother appears, the doorman at Harrods puts the entire staff on full alert and junior sales staff go off sick in droves. Daddy gets so embarrassed. He's so sweet and gentle and he hates the way Mummy talks to people.'

'Yes,' Janine agreed, 'my dad's the same. Sometimes on Saturday mornings he hides in the shed so he doesn't have to go shopping with her. I wish he was here now. Sometimes he can calm her down a bit, but I don't suppose Mum's even bothered to ring him.'

'I could do that later if you give me his number,' Ollie volunteered.

'Better not,' Janine said quietly, 'I don't suppose Mum would like it if I went behind her back.'

'Whatever you say. Could you turn towards me a little, so I can get at your face? What does your father do?'

'He's a draughtsman, but he should have

been an artist. He's really talented, does brilliant watercolours, but he's also an incredible cartoonist. Dad wanted to go to art college but Granddad thought that was too frivolous, so now Dad spends his days drawing boring things like stanchions, when what he should really be doing is creating wonderful things.'

Ollie finished cleaning off the grazes and put gauze pads over the wounds before she removed her gloves. 'Just hold still a moment until I've taped those down. Do you take after him? Can you draw?'

'A bit.'

As Ollie cut two short strips of tape and stuck down the dressing on Janine's cheek, she couldn't help noticing the guarded look which came into the girl's eyes. 'I can't even draw square boxes in perspective,' Ollie admitted. 'What sort of thing do you do?'

'I used to do portraits mostly.'

'Used to?'

Janine said bitterly 'Mum doesn't exactly approve of either of us scribbling, as she calls it.'

'There, you're just about done for now,' Ollie said as she put the scissors back on the trolley and tidied up. 'I hope you won't have to wait too long for X-ray . Is there anything I can get you?'

'There is one thing,' Janine said with some hesitation, 'which might help pass the time.'

'What's that?'

'In my bag, at the very bottom, there's a pencil case and a sketch pad. Do you think I could have them?'

'Yes, of course.'

Ollie bent down and unzipped Janine's bag.

'It's underneath all the clothes and shoes. I hide it because Mum doesn't really like me carrying it around with me. She says it's a distraction, but I find it relaxing to draw when I'm sitting around waiting in rehearsals.'

While she was searching for the pad, Ollie noticed several containers of pills. Quickly reading the labels, she discovered they were all different types of laxatives. She also knew that they had not been prescribed by a doctor, but were the sort which could be bought easily in any chemist's shop.

Janine, thinking it was taking Ollie a long time, asked, 'Haven't you found the pad yet?'

Hastily taking out the pad and pencil case, Ollie handed them to the girl. 'Here you are. May I see some of your work?'

But Janine kept her hand firmly on the closed book. 'There's nothing much in here, really.'

'OK,' Ollie shrugged and walked towards the curtains.

Janine realised she'd been rather rude. She called after Ollie. 'If I do something worth seeing, maybe I could show you later.'

Ollie smiled. 'I'll look forward to that.' But as soon as she was out of the cubicle Ollie's thoughts returned to the worrying quantity of laxatives she'd found hidden away amongst the girl's belongings. She shook her head. No normal, healthy young person should ever need all those!

5

'ARE YOU THE ONLY ONE out here?' Vee asked, as she met Ollie scuttling between cubicles carrying a disposable urine bottle.

'At the moment, yes. Everyone else is in Crash sorting out the RTA.'

'In that case,' Vee said, 'you ought to know, there's an old man in cubicle three who's pulled his dressing off and he's bleeding all over the floor.'

'Oh, no!' Ollie said fiercely. 'I've already put that back on twice. I'll be there in a minute.'

'Nurse!' an anguished male voice cried from behind a cubicle curtain. 'I can't hold it much longer!'

'Coming,' Ollie called back to him, before asking Vee, 'Have you seen a domestic anywhere?'

'Not for a while.'

'Well, when you do, could you ask them to mop up the floor in three before someone slips.'

'NURSE!'

'I'll do the floor,' Vee offered, 'while you sort him out.'

'Thanks, Vee,' Ollie said and disappeared into the cubicle.

'Where's the mobile X-ray?' Angus asked, as he continued to examine the injured driver in Crash.

'They're on their way,' Sister Broadhurst said.

Angus lifted the girl's eyelids and shone a torch into each eye. Both had bruising around them. 'She's got racoon eyes. Possible basal skull fracture. What's her name?'

'According to her driving licence,' Ba said, 'Lesley.'

'Lesley!' Angus repeated the name loudly, 'Lesley, can you hear me?'

But the girl showed no sign of response.

'What about a Venflon?' Angus asked.

'It's already in,' Jill responded.

'Thanks, Nurse,' he smiled and then, as he glanced at the ECG monitor, his expression rapidly changed. 'She's gone into ventricular fibrillation.'

Sister Broadhurst immediately began regular cardiopulmonary resuscitation. Jill quickly smeared the conducting gel, which would help electrical contact, across Lesley's chest. Ba handed Angus the defibrillator paddles. He applied one paddle to the girl's sternum and the other to the apex of her heart. 'Two hundred joules, please. Everybody off!' He flicked the switches on the paddle handles. The shock was delivered and her body jerked as the muscles violently contracted.

'No response,' Tarquin said quietly.

'Going again,' Angus said while the machine recharged. 'Everybody off.' Again the body jerked.

Tarquin shook his head. 'Still nothing.'

'One milligram of adrenaline, Tarquin.'

Tarquin injected the substance through the Venflon which gave direct access to a vein in Lesley's arm.

'Come on, Lesley!' Angus muttered under his breath. 'I'll go to three hundred and sixty joules this time,' he said, biting his lower lip. 'Everybody off!'

For the third time Lesley's body reacted, and after a pause, Tarquin said, 'She's back.'

Angus nodded. 'Good girl, Lesley! Give her a hundred milligrams of lignocaine.'

The silence which followed their activities

was suddenly broken by the muffled ringing of a telephone.

'Where the hell is that coming from?' Angus demanded.

Everybody looked round, but nobody could locate the source of the persistent ringing. Then Jill opened the plastic bag containing Lesley's personal belongings. 'She's got a mobile phone in her bag.'

'Then switch the damn thing off quick,' Angus snapped, 'before it interferes with every life-support machine in the building!' Jill silenced the phone and Angus relaxed. 'Now, let's see what needs to be done for this young lady.'

During a breathing space, Ollie decided to risk exposing herself to Mrs Connolly's displeasure. She had hardly set foot in reception before Mrs Connolly spotted her and advanced. Ollie decided attack would be the best form of defence. 'Before you ask, Mrs Connolly, I haven't yet been able to find anyone free to speak to you, but I haven't forgotten.'

'It really isn't good enough,' Mrs Connolly fretted. 'When Mrs Armstrong's Serena went to the Sports Injury Clinic she was seen and treated immediately.'

Trying to be as reasonable as possible, because she was hoping to get some information out of Janine's mother, Ollie carefully suggested, 'But most people go to that sort of clinic with appointments, Mrs Connolly, just like our clinics. This department is set up to respond instantly to the unexpected, particularly when someone's life is at stake. How would you feel if it was your daughter they'd cut out of that car, whose life was in immediate danger, and we told you she'd have to wait in the queue behind the cut fingers and broken legs for treatment?'

Mrs Connolly reluctantly began to give way. 'Yes, I understand.'

'We won't keep Janine waiting a second longer than necessary and she is quite comfortable.'

'Why can't I see her?'

'She's sleeping at the moment,' Ollie lied, knowing that Janine would rest more easily without her mother fussing round her. 'But I'll come and collect you the moment she wakes up. Incidentally, just before she dropped off, Janine wondered if you'd phoned her father?'

Mrs Connolly looked quite surprised. 'What on earth for?'

'To let him know what's happened.'

'But Dan's at work. He won't want to be bothered with something like this.'

Ollie, who had a distinct feeling from the way Janine had spoken about her parents that Mr Connolly would have a more positive effect on his daughter than her mother had, wasn't prepared to give up. 'Janine would like him to know. You'll find some telephones next to the coffee machine.'

'Oh, very well.'

'There is just one other thing,' Ollie added, trying to make it sound like an afterthought. 'Is your daughter on any kind of medication or special diet?'

'She's not taking any medicines,' Mrs Connolly said proudly. 'Janine's always been a very healthy girl.'

'And what about diet?'

'Well, obviously all dancers have to be careful about their weight.'

Ollie persisted. 'But she eats normally?'

'She avoids starchy and fatty foods, but apart from that she does, yes.' Mrs Connolly frowned. 'Why are you asking all these questions?'

'Well, when we see someone every day, it's often difficult to spot physical changes in them and we're less likely to notice changes of habit, like loss of appetite. You haven't noticed anything like that with Janine?'

'I don't think so.'

'And she has been quite well?'

'Well, yes, of course, otherwise I would have done something about it,' Mrs Connolly said emphatically, but then her tone suddenly changed. 'Mind you, just lately she's been complaining of tiredness. I keep telling her she has too many late nights.'

'A typical teenager,' Ollie smiled. 'I was just the same. Of course, when I was Janine's age, I was at boarding school but, whenever I got the chance, I used to stay out all hours with boyfriends and wonder why I couldn't get up the next day.'

Mrs Connolly was shocked. 'Oh, she doesn't do anything like that!'

'But Janine's a very attractive girl,' Ollie pointed out. 'I would have thought she'd have stacks of boyfriends at her age.'

'Oh, no,' Mrs Connolly said firmly. 'We don't allow that sort of thing. We've told her there'll be time enough for that later. Just for now she has to concentrate on her dancing. No, what I meant about late nights was sitting up watching television. For instance, only last night she was up until half-past nine.'

Poor kid, Ollie thought, what a rotten life!

Mrs Connolly looked serious. 'Why are you asking all these questions? I don't see what any of this has to do with having a broken leg.'

'Oh, nothing,' Ollie agreed. 'They're just general questions about her health and well-being.'

'I'm happy to say there's nothing to fear in that department,' Mrs Connolly said confidently.

If only you knew, Ollie thought and then, just before she left she reminded Mrs Connolly. 'You won't forget to ring your husband, will you?'

'I'll do it now,' Mrs Connolly assured her, 'and you'll come and get me as soon as Janine wakes up, won't you?'

'Yes, of course.'

'And,' Mrs Connolly paused and looked uncomfortable before she blurted out, 'I'm sorry if I was a little short with you earlier. It's only that I was worried about my daughter.'

'Don't worry, Mrs Connolly,' Ollie said. 'I do understand.'

As Ollie passed the desk, Maureen said, 'I've

had Alexander on the phone again for you twice.'

'I really am sorry. Look, if he bothers you again, tell him to go and boil his head.'

Maureen nodded. 'Now that would be an interesting piece of advice to come from a receptionist in Accident and Emergency. Which reminds me,' she added, nodding towards the occupied rows of seats, 'the natives are getting restless.'

Ollie took the sheaf of casualty cards from the tray. 'I'll go and check how things are going.'

Dean and another porter came out of Crash wheeling Lesley's trolley towards the lift, on the way up to an operating theatre.

As Margery Broadhurst and Ba emerged together, Margery asked, 'How's Nurse Smith shaping up?'

'It's early to say yet, she's still finding her way round, but she seems to have her wits about her.'

Sister Broadhurst looked unconvinced. 'I simply can't believe someone who turns up an hour late on her first day in a new job can possibly have the kind of dedication this job demands.'

Ba enquired, 'Did you ask her why she was late?'

Margery shook her head. 'I was too angry at the time and when she turned up with all that luggage and asked if she could take the morning off to go and look for somewhere to live, well, that was the final straw.'

'I know what you mean,' Ba conceded, 'but she certainly got stuck in once she was here and she does keep her eyes open. While we were undressing that girl with the fractured tibia, it was Nurse Smith who noticed how thin she was and suggested the possibility of anorexia.'

Margery sniffed. 'Probably an overreaction. It's a very fashionable problem these days and far too easy to jump to that conclusion.'

'Well, in this particular case I'm not so sure,' Ba said. 'Anyway, I've asked Ollie to pursue it gently and see what she can find out by talking to the girl.' At that moment Ba happened to spot Ollie returning from reception with the cards. 'Lets see how she's getting on. Ollie!'

'There's quite a backlog of patients waiting in reception,' Ollie reported to Sister Broadhurst, 'though nothing too serious. I've prioritised the cas. cards.'

But unfortunately, as Ollie tried to hand over the cards to Sister, somehow their hands didn't quite meet and the neatly organised stack of cards cascaded to the floor.

'What a shame they didn't stay that way,' Sister Broadhurst observed tartly as, for the second time that day, Ollie ended up scrabbling round on her hands and knees at Sister's feet, picking up the pieces.

'I'm sorry,' Ollie apologised, while handing over the confused handful.

'Next time,' Sister said acidly, 'just shuffle the cards and we'll take the first patient you happen to deal off the top!'

'I really am sorry,' Ollie insisted, reddening with annoyance at her own clumsiness.

Ba intervened quickly. 'Ollie, have you been able to get any more out of Janine?'

'I discovered she's got a large quantity of laxatives stashed away in her bag,' Ollie reported.

Margery Broadhurst couldn't believe what she was hearing. 'You mean you went rummaging through a patient's personal belongings?'

'No, not at all,' Ollie quickly explained 'Janine asked me to get something from her bag and I happened to notice several containers of different laxatives. Far more than anyone like her should need and they'd been bought over the counter, not prescribed by a doctor. Also, her mother says Janine constantly complains of tiredness even after normal amounts of rest.'

Sister Broadhurst fixed Ollie with a quizzical look. 'You mean, without talking to a doctor, you've already discussed your theory with Janine's mother?'

'Certainly not.'

'Well, that's a relief,' Sister Broadhurst said. 'After all, so far it's mostly speculation.'

Ollie flushed. 'I think it's a little more than that.'

But Margery Broadhurst was not giving any ground. 'Your theory may possibly be right, but it's too early to trigger off a whole series of precautionary measures on such slender evidence. Do what you've been doing. Keep asking questions with your eyes, ears and, most important of all, your mind open. But report any findings to Staff Nurse Heywood or to me first. Is that understood?'

Ollie, feeling her efforts weren't being appreciated, bit back an angry retort and said, 'Yes, Sister.'

As Margery turned to leave, she added, 'And

please do something with that dreadful hair of yours!'

'It makes me sick!' Ollie said to Ba as she stabbed her hair back into place.

'What does?'

'Sister treats me like a stupid child,' Ollie grumbled. 'She's more interested in my hair than what's going on in my head.'

'I don't think that's true,' Ba said calmly. 'As for treating you like a child, you are young enough to be her daughter. Besides which, you didn't exactly impress Sister Broadhurst by turning up late, or by depositing a pile of cas. cards at her feet. Incidentally, I didn't mention it at the time, but I'm sure one drifted away under that trolley.'

Ollie knelt down to retrieve it. 'Oh, no! You're right. Fortunately nothing more serious than a man with a boil on his bum – he could easily have got it lanced by his own GP anyway. The trouble is, when I make mistakes I always do it in front of people like Sister. The only time in my life I've dropped a tureen full of soup, it had to land on my headmistress's toe.'

'But as far as your ideas about Janine go,' Ba continued, 'Sister didn't dismiss them: she just isn't convinced that what you've discovered so far is conclusive. If she thought you were entirely on the wrong tack, she would simply have told you to drop the whole thing, which she didn't.'

Ollie sighed. 'I suppose you're right.'

'I think you've just got to keep talking to Janine, and her mother, and get everything out of them you can. Particularly the girl. After all, if Janine is anorexic, there isn't anything we can do for her unless she's willing to face up to the fact. She isn't a child either and its impossible to treat somebody who doesn't believe that they are ill.'

'OK, I'll keep trying.'

'Good,' Ba smiled, 'but let's catch up with some of the other patients too.'

'So where are we now?' Tarquin asked, passing his hand wearily through his hair as he checked the status board.

Sister Broadhurst brought him up to date. 'There's a man with a cut on his head in three. The pregnant woman's still waiting for the results of her blood and urine tests. We've also got a child who's supposed to have swallowed a wedding ring but flatly refuses to say one way or the other. There's certainly no obvious airway obstruction. Shall we send that one straight to X-ray?'

'Yes, why not? What else?'

'There's the other two young men from the traffic accident. Grit in an eye in six and ambulance control have just rung to say they are bringing a child in with a needle through her hand.'

'Oh, well, it all sounds about par for the course,' Tarquin said with a tired smile. 'I think I might go and grab a sandwich while I've got the chance.'

'I was going to ask, Doctor,' Margery interrupted 'What's your impression of our latest recruit?'

'Nurse Smith?' Tarquin shrugged. 'Seems competent enough.'

'Yes,' Margery sighed, 'but what about that hair?'

'It is rather fantastic, isn't it?' Tarquin said with relish, entirely missing the point Sister was making. 'Like a lion's mane.'

'That wasn't quite what I meant,' Sister Broadhurst said heavily. Sometimes she began to wonder if she was the only person left in the entire hospital with any real standards. 'Do you think,' she enquired tartly, 'your sandwich could wait until we catch up a little?'

'I already feel as if it's two days since I last ate, so what's a few more hours?'

Ignoring Tarquin's sarcasm, she continued, 'Then shall we take a look at the man with the bleeding head?'

'Janine,' Ollie said, as she opened the curtains.

Startled, Janine, like someone half her age caught doing something wicked, tried to hide the pad and pencil.

'Sorry to make you jump,' Ollie apologised, 'but at long last, they're ready for you in X-ray. Dean will take you there in a moment. How's the drawing going?'

'It's not very good.'

Ollie smiled. 'I bet it is. May I see it?'

'Can't you wait until it's finished?'

'I'm used to looking at work in progress,' Ollie said reassuringly. 'I've got a couple of friends who are artists.'

Janine looked at her wide-eyed. 'Real ones?'

'Yes, of course. Anton's very successful and he's got a studio in Paris.'

Janine put her head on one side and gazed longingly into the distance. 'That sounds so romantic.'

'It is when the sun's shining and plenty of

tourists turn up to buy things,' Ollie admitted. 'Come on then, let's have a look.'

'It's really only a rough sketch,' Janine apologised in advance, hugging the pad close to her chest. 'I'm sure it's nowhere near as good as something your friends could do.'

'Let me see,' Ollie insisted. She took the pad and found she was looking at an excellent portrait of herself. 'This is terribly good. You're really talented. You've even got my Medusa-like hair!'

Janine looked baffled. 'Medusa?'

'You know, the Greek woman with snakes for hair. I often think I'd be better off with a snake-charmer instead of a hair drier. This drawing's really good though.'

'Do you think so – honest?' Janine was pleased by the compliment. 'You can have it when I've finished, if you like.'

Before Ollie had a chance to thank Janine, Dean arrived with a wheelchair to take her to X-ray.

'Are you coming too?' Janine asked, hopefully, as they carefully lifted her off the bed.

'No, but I'll be here when you get back,' Ollie assured her.

Dean, scenting the possibility of an easy touch

with a new member of staff, was more interested in Nurse Smith than the patient. 'I don't suppose you could lend me a fiver? Only I haven't eaten today and I've left my wallet at home.'

But Ollie, who'd been conned by experts, wasn't interested. 'Sorry, I haven't got a penny on me.'

'Oh, well, you can't blame a bloke for trying,' Dean moaned.

'And, Janine, when you get back, I'd like to weigh you.'

Janine shot a look at Ollie. 'Weigh me? Why do you want to do that?'

Ollie smiled. 'Standard procedure.'

'But I weigh myself every day,' Janine protested. 'I can tell you my exact weight if you want to write it down.

'It's no trouble,' Ollie said firmly, 'because our scales are more accurate than your average bathroom scales.'

'You could weigh me as well,' Dean grumbled. 'I'm sure I'm losing weight with not eating regular.'

Taking in Dean's ample girth, Ollie observed, 'I suspect you could live off your fat for a fortnight.'

'Thanks a bunch,' Dean said gloomily, as he

wheeled the chair down the corridor.

But Ollie was still thinking about Janine's drawing. She certainly wasn't just a scribbler.'

6

'WHY DIDN'T YOU ring me sooner?' Mr Connolly demanded, when he eventually joined his wife in Accident and Emergency reception. A chubby little man in a dusty, ill-fitting grey suit, he looked anxiously at his wife through spectacles held together by sticky tape. 'You didn't have to go through all this alone. You must have been worried sick.'

'Dan, I thought you'd be far too busy to do anything,' his wife replied, but as she spoke, she seemed uncomfortable and avoided his gaze.

'I've tried to tell you a hundred times,' Dan said, shaking his head in disbelief, 'I'd drop anything if either of you needed me. How did it happen?'

Mrs Connolly went through the events of the morning in detail. 'But now there's been this long delay. The nurse told me it was because they had to deal with some people from a traffic accident, but I'm not sure I believe her.'

'Why on earth shouldn't you believe her?' Dan asked in amazement. 'Do you think they all went off to a party somewhere and left you sitting here?'

Mrs Connolly gripped his arm. 'I think something terrible might have happened to Janine and they're not telling me.' As she finished speaking, Mrs Connolly closed her eyes but not quickly enough to prevent a tear from escaping and trickling slowly down her cheek.

Dan put his arm round his wife's shoulders. 'Mary, you worry yourself sick about that girl. You always have, ever since the day she was born. I'll never forget the night we brought her home from the maternity hospital. I couldn't convince you the baby alarm was working properly and you were up and down those stairs all evening to make sure she was still breathing. I remember waking up at about three o'clock in the morning and finding you sitting right beside her cot.'

'You thought I was being silly.'

Dan smiled gently, 'Only because you'd been sitting there so long, you'd fallen fast asleep. If anything really had happened to Janine, nothing short of an earthquake would have woken you anyway. You've fussed over her all her life,' Dan insisted, 'always convinced disaster was waiting to strike.'

'Well,' Mrs Connolly said, 'Janine is our only child.'

'But you imagine all kinds of problems where none exist. Like now. I mean, a broken leg is a broken leg. What could possibly go wrong?'

'I don't know, but the longer I sit here, the worse things I imagine.'

'Why don't I get us both a cup of tea?'

'I'll do it.'

'Mary, I can get two cups of tea. I get it myself several times a day at work with no ill effects. Where's the machine?'

'Oh, let me.' And she was gone before he could protest. As she returned, Ollie emerged and Mrs Connolly's hands started to shake. 'Yes, Nurse, what is it? Has something happened?'

'Hello, you must be Mr Connolly,' Ollie said with a smile.

'Yes,' Dan said, hastily taking the cups from his wife's hands before she spilled hot tea over herself.

'Is anything wrong?' Mrs Connolly insisted.

'Nothing's the matter,' Ollie assured them both. 'I simply came to tell you your daughter has gone to X-ray now and as soon as she's back, I'll come and get you. All right?'

'Thank you, yes.'

* * *

When Ollie returned to the unit, Ba asked, 'Have you had a break yet?'

Ollie shook her head. 'But I'm fine.'

'Now that things have calmed down,' Ba suggested, 'why don't you pop into the staff room and make yourself a drink?'

'But I want to be here to weigh Janine when she comes back.'

'If you aren't back by then, I'll weigh her and then I'll call you,' Ba promised.

Ollie went upstairs and found the staff room empty. She filled the jug kettle and, while it was boiling washed up some mugs, took milk from the fridge and was just reaching into the cupboard for a jar of instant coffee when Jill came in and snapped, 'That coffee's mine.'

'I'm sorry,' Ollie apologised, 'I didn't realise.'

'My name's on the lid.'

'Like I say, I'm sorry,' Ollie said, handing the jar to Jill. 'I hadn't got as far as seeing the name on it.'

'Coffee's expensive and people are always nicking stuff out of the cupboard.'

Jill proceeded to make herself coffee and Ollie couldn't help noticing that, without a word of thanks, Jill was quite happy to use one of the mugs she'd washed and take water from the kettle Ollie had boiled. 'If I'd known the system,' Ollie chattered on, 'I'd have brought some with me. I'm in such a muddle, I haven't even arranged anywhere to stay yet. Could I borrow some of your coffee and pay you back tomorrow?'

'I suppose,' Jill mumbled, but far from offering to make coffee for Ollie, she shoved the jar towards her. 'Just make sure you put it back on the shelf when you've finished.'

'Don't worry, I will.'

Jill sat in a corner sipping her coffee and watching Ollie. 'I hear you did your training in London.'

'That's right,' Ollie replied, but sensing Jill's antagonism, she took her drink and sat on the opposite side of the room.

'So why didn't you stay there?' Jill asked bluntly.

'I'd love to have stayed in London,' Ollie admitted. 'All my friends are there and there are so many exciting things to do. It'll be a big change coming here.'

'Then why did you?' Jill asked pointedly, wondering if she would admit to the scandal Vee had hinted at.

'I wasn't given the choice,' Ollie confessed.

Searching for the slightest sign of guilt, Jill's eyes never left Ollie's face as she continued to press her. 'Something you did wrong?'

'Not exactly. Hey, why are you giving me the third degree?'

'No particular reason,' Jill said.

Vee breezed into the room, 'Hi, kids. Any hot water in the kettle? I've got myself a pot-noodle.'

'There is,' Jill said flatly, angrily tossing the remains of her coffee into the sink, 'if she hasn't used it all.'

As the door closed behind Jill, puzzled by her belligerent attitude, Ollie asked, 'What's rattled her cage?'

'Don't take too much notice,' Vee said as she added water and stirred the contents with her pen. 'Jill sees you as a rival.'

'A rival – for what?'

'Firstly for Tarquin.'

'She's welcome to him!' Ollie declared. 'I wouldn't trust him farther than I could hurl him!'

'But secondly, for what she thinks of as her job. Having trained here, at the end of her six months, she was hoping she might get another contract, if not a permanency. Now you've

turned up, she thinks it might be more difficult.'

Ollie nodded. 'I see. That explains why she
was asking me all kinds of questions about my
murky past.'

'Oooh, do tell!' Vee said enthusiastically
rubbing her hands together. Maybe her friend
Tina hadn't been exaggerating!

'Where would you like me to start?' Ollie
laughed. 'How about the fact that I was thrown
out of three schools. Well, four actually, if you
count Marlborough.'

'Isn't Marlborough a boy's school?'

'Yes, that was why I got thrown out. I was
caught climbing into one of the dormitories at
about midnight one night!'

Vee's eyes widened. 'Ollie!'

'I only did it for a bet,' Ollie claimed.

'Honest?'

'Yes, mind you,' Ollie remembered wistfully,
'at the time they did have an incredibly rich and
good-looking Arabian prince in the sixth form.'

'That sounds more like it!' Vee laughed,
though she was shaking her head in disbelief.
'You know, if I did anything like that, my family would have me locked away in a nunnery by
the end of the week.'

'Really?'

'They're very religious and I had a very strict upbringing.'

'Well, most of the stories about my chequered past have all been embroidered beyond belief. Like the time I ran away to Paris from the Swiss finishing school my mother dumped me in. Rumours that I'd absconded with the entire French rugby team were a gross exaggeration.'

'Were they?'

Ollie grinned from ear to ear. 'Well, slightly.'

'You,' Vee was laughing so much she had to fight to get the words out, 'are totally outrageous.'

Ollie shook her head, innocently bewildered by the romantic complications of her own life. 'I don't know how these things happen to me, but they do, all the time. Look at the way Tarquin started hitting on me the minute I walked through the door.'

Vee asked, 'Hey, Ollie, have you got anywhere to stay yet?'

Ollie came rapidly down to earth. 'Oh, no! I knew there was something I meant to do the minute I had a break. There isn't going to be time now. I suppose I'll have to stay in some grotty bed and breakfast dump.'

Vee observed, 'I would have thought you'd be going to the Grand Hotel at the very least.'

'On a nurse's pay – you must be joking! Mummy and Daddy paid for my education right up to that Swiss finishing school, but when I still insisted on being a nurse, Mummy made sure I was cut off without a penny. Daddy sometimes smuggles out the odd cheque, but he's so gaga, he usually sends them to the wrong address. No, I can assure you, I may have a cut-glass accent, but it's nail varnish stopping the runs in my tights most of the time.'

'Well, look,' Vee said warmly, 'the offer I made this morning stills stands. I've got this massive flat in an old warehouse down by the docks. I know it doesn't sound much, but there are four bedrooms and you're welcome to stay.'

'That's fantastically kind of you.'

'To be honest,' Vee said, 'I'd be glad of the company. I only moved in a couple of weeks ago. The girl I was going to share with got a job in Bristol, and I rattle round in there like a pea in a tin can. I tell you what, you don't have to commit yourself. Stay tonight, while you get yourself sorted, and as long as you like, but if you hate it, we don't get on or you find somewhere you like better, you go and no hard feelings. How's that?'

'Amazing, thanks,' Ollie said, 'but what about money?'

'We'll sort all that out,' Vee said with a happy grin, delighted that she was going to have some company, 'but don't worry. After what you said, I won't bleed you dry. I know now, you're nothing but poor white trash!'

Their laughter was interrupted by Ba. 'Nurse Smith, I sent you up here for a short break, not a three-course meal.'

'Sorry, Staff.'

'Janine's back with her X-rays. Tarquin says there are no complications. It's an oblique fracture of the tibia but there's no dislocation so she can go to the plaster room for a full leg cylinder. Her parents are in with her at the moment, but once the plaster's on, she'll be ready for discharge. So I think it's now or never time, if you're going to get anywhere with this anorexia business. I have weighed her. She's down to ninety pounds.'

'Ninety!'

Ba nodded as she poured herself coffee. 'Exactly. I tell you what, go with her to the plaster room, then you can talk to her while she's having the cast put on. But, look Ollie,' Ba added, 'don't be too hard on yourself if you don't get anywhere with this. Remember, she only came in with a broken leg.'

'But if she has a much greater problem,' Ollie said, with quiet determination, 'we can't just let her leave without doing something about it.'

'If possible, yes,' Ba pointed out, 'but in the end we can only treat the symptoms people are willing to share with us. I suspect that Janine already has an inkling that you're on to her and she may clam up altogether. All I'm saying, Ollie, is that you mustn't blame yourself if this doesn't work out. It is an outside chance.'

'I'll do my best.'

Ollie left the staff room and, as there was nobody about and she was in a hurry to get back to tackling Janine, she climbed on to the banister and slid down, riding it side-saddle.

Unfortunately, at the bottom of the stairs, she couldn't stop herself, and went full tilt into Dean who was carrying a stack of metal kidney dishes back to the unit.

The dishes spun out of his hands and landed with a loud clatter on the tiled floor. The noise of the crash echoed up the stairwell which made it twice as loud and last twice as long.

'Thanks a bunch!' Dean grumbled, as he picked up the dishes. 'Now they'll all need sterilising again.'

'Sorry, Dean,' Ollie said with a sheepish grin.

Suddenly the door to the unit flew open, revealing Sister Broadhurst. 'What's all the noise?'

'Sorry, Sister, it was my fault,' Ollie apologised. 'I had a slight accident.'

Sister Broadhurst drew herself up, 'We've got enough accidents in here with the patients; we don't need any more. Get back on the unit immediately.'

'Yes, Sister.'

7

'ARE MY RESULTS still not back?' Sarah asked anxiously.

'I'm sure they won't be long now,' Jill said, checking Sarah's temperature again and noting it was higher.

'I wish I'd remembered the cat food.'

Jill smiled. She was used to distressed patients' minds wandering off at complete tangents. 'How many cats have you got?'

'Six. They were all strays I sort of adopted as kittens,' Sarah explained. 'I love them, but Aidan thinks the only reason I started to collect them was because we were having trouble having a baby. He thinks they're my consolation prize.'

'You'll have a huge family soon then,' Jill observed.

'I hope so,' Sarah said, tears welling up in her eyes again, 'but this one inside me is the most important of all.'

'I'll go and see if those results are through yet,' Jill said, and left in search of Angus, who she found with Tarquin. 'Have you seen the results of Sarah's blood and urine tests yet?' she asked. Angus shook his head. 'Only, she's getting very upset and her temperature's still rising.'

'I saw her notes,' Tarquin intervened. Probably nothing more than glandular fever and she'll end up with a mild case of jaundice.'

Angus glanced sternly at Tarquin. 'Possibly, but until we're certain, there's always a need to keep a close eye on any older woman who's having her first baby.'

'Mr McFee,' Jill said, 'while I was talking to Sarah she did mention she had six cats.'

Angus's eyebrows rose. 'Cats?'

The moment she parted the cubicle curtains, Ollie immediately took in the family group. Although Mrs Connolly was sitting right beside Janine and holding her hand, the girl's eyes never left her father's face. Ollie also couldn't help noticing there was no sign of Janine's drawing pad. She must have persuaded Dean to stow it away before her parents arrived.

Before she took Janine to the plaster room, for what might be their last conversation together, Ollie decided to take advantage of

Mrs Connolly's being so wrapped up in her daughter to get a word, alone, with her father. 'Excuse me.' As Ollie spoke, all three turned to look at her. 'Mr Connolly, might I have a brief word?'

Ollie was keenly aware of the look of disappointment that flashed across Janine's face as she took the girl's father out into the corridor, but Mrs Connolly was still too busy talking to notice.

When they were outside, Mr Connolly asked, 'Yes, Nurse, what is it?'

'I'm a little worried about your daughter, Mr Connolly.'

'Is it her leg? The doctor said—'

'No,' Ollie interrupted to reassure him, 'it's not her leg. That's going to be perfectly all right. But I did wonder how she'll cope with being in plaster?'

'You mean getting about, that sort of thing? Well, my wife will look after all that.'

'No, I was really thinking, how is Janine going to fill her time if she can't dance?'

'We hadn't thought about that yet.'

'Talking to her earlier,' Ollie pressed on while he considered the problem, 'Janine told me she used to draw quite a bit and, of course, that would be an ideal way of passing the time for someone who isn't very mobile.'

Doubt crossed his face. It reminded Ollie of the hunted expression which Janine had displayed while they were discussing the same subject. 'I'm not sure that's a very good idea.'

'She told me you're quite an artist yourself.'

Mr Connolly looked modest and rather shy. 'I'm a draughtsman.'

'But Janine said you do wonderful water colours and you're a brilliant cartoonist.

'Oh, that was years ago when I was young. Now, I only do the occasional painting in the holidays.'

'You never thought of taking it up professionally?' Ollie enquired innocently.

A brief shadow of memory flitted across his face before he dismissed the suggestion, just as his father had done years ago. 'It wasn't practical. There's too much competition. At least with technical drawing there's always an outlet. Although computers are rapidly taking over.'

'But it's your talent Janine inherited,' Ollie said, 'and I'm surprised you didn't encourage her.'

Mr Connolly looked uncomfortable. 'It was just that, from when she was a little girl, Janine was such a good dancer and Mary, my wife, thought that was what she ought to do.'

'And Janine agreed?'

'Well, she was only tiny.'

A new thought suddenly struck Ollie. 'Is Mrs Connolly a good dancer?'

'Oh, yes, my wife won cups – though that was for ballroom dancing,' Mr Connolly said proudly. 'Mind you, that was before we met. I don't dance. I've got two left feet and no sense of rhythm.'

'I still think,' Ollie persisted, 'while she's immobilised, Janine might enjoy some encouragement with her drawing.'

'Well, we'll see,' Mr Connolly said uncertainly, 'but there's always reading and things.'

'Just an idea,' Ollie said. 'We'd better get the plaster put on now and then you can take her home.'

Looking puzzled, Sister Broadhurst hung up the phone and turned to Ba. 'Where's Nurse Smith?'

'In the plaster room with Janine Connolly. Why?'

'I've just had Sir Richard Askins on the phone.'

Ba was no wiser. 'Who's he?'

'A member of the management board,' Margery Broadhurst explained sarcastically. 'One of those businessmen with no knowledge or experience of medicine who they appoint at great expense to show us how easy it is to stay in budget.'

'What's that got to do with Ollie?'

Sister Broadhurst shook her head. 'I dread to think, but he said he's coming down to see her later and when anyone from management ventures this far, it can only mean one thing – trouble.'

'Poor kid! But what on earth can she have done?' Ba asked. 'She not been here a day yet.'

'I suppose somebody with a good deal of clout must have complained. Can you think who it might be?'

'Mrs Connolly got a bit upset at being kept waiting,' Ba said. 'But most of the patients seem to like her.'

'Oh well,' Sister Broadhurst said, 'we'll find out soon enough. He's coming down before the end of the shift. We'd better make sure everything's as it should be, just in case he goes poking about. Not that he'd know a splint from a broom handle!'

'Shall I get Vee to iron all the cubicle curtains and polish the fire-extinguishers?' Bee asked, with a wry smile.

'That sort of thing, yes,' Margery Broadhurst said with a deep sigh, 'and while you're about it, make sure there are no paper clips missing.'

'And definitely,' Ba said, getting into the spirit of the thing, 'no patients bleeding all over the place and making it look untidy!'

'In fact it would be better if there weren't any patients,' Sister said. 'Just think, we could manage a one hundred per cent efficiency rate without them.'

In the plaster room, having carefully removed the splint from Janine's leg, a senior staff nurse explained, 'I'm going to do your cast in two parts, below the knee first to immobilise the fracture.' She wound a layer from a wide cotton-wool roll round the leg. 'When the final cast's on, this cotton wool will extend beyond the cast, to stop your skin rubbing against the edges.'

Staff dunked the plaster roll in a plastic bowl of warm water and gave Janine last-minute instructions. 'Just keep the knee very slightly bent and your foot at right angles to the leg,

OK? It's very important that you keep perfectly still during this, so that it goes on correctly.'

'Your feet aren't ticklish, are they Janine?' Ollie asked.

'No,' Janine laughed. 'After years of dancing, they've got skin like rhino hide.'

'That's a relief. When I was practising plastering during my training, I was given a patient who was so ticklish we ended up with plaster everywhere. All over me, the walls and ceiling. In fact, everywhere but on him.'

'How long does it take to set?' Janine asked the staff nurse.

'Forty-eight hours to set completely and it's very important you don't put any weight on it until then, otherwise we'll be back to square one.'

'So how do I get about?'

Ollie said cheerfully, 'On crutches. We throw in an eye-patch and a stuffed parrot for no extra charge.'

'Having crutches could be fun.'

'Not if you try them out on a polished floor, or a flight of stairs, believe me. I made that mistake once after a skiing accident and nearly broke my neck. My ski instructor gave me a certificate which looked like a police summons. It said I was guilty of being drunk in charge of a plaster cast. He was miffed because I'd almost brained him with the cast.'

While the nurse concentrated on applying the plaster, Ollie said casually, 'I noticed from your chart that you are very underweight.' Janine's leg twitched. 'Keep still!'

Janine instantly went on the defensive. 'I've got a very light frame.'

'How tall are you?'

'About five foot four.'

'OK, so at your age and height your average weight should be between a hundred and twenty and a hundred and thirty pounds. You're well below that.'

Janine didn't reply, but abruptly turned her head away. Although Ollie couldn't see Janine's facial reaction, she was aware of the girl's body stiffening slightly, as if she were bracing herself to resist further attack from Ollie. But having got that far, Ollie felt she could only press on. 'In your bag you've got a lot of laxatives.'

Janine swung her read round and glared at Ollie. 'You had no right to go nosing through my belongings!'

'I didn't. I happened to see them when you asked me to get your drawing things out. The point is, unless you have some kind of illness, you couldn't possibly need laxatives, and certainly not in those quantities.'

'The doctor gave them to me.'

'Which doctor? Your GP?' Ollie asked, but when Janine didn't reply, she carried on. 'They weren't prescribed by a doctor or they'd have the doctor's label on them. You bought them at the chemist's. Don't you realise, if you use laxatives over a prolonged period of time, they can cause all kinds of problems. Anything from diarrhoea to a serious chemical imbalance in the blood. Some types of laxative coat the intestine which reduces vitamin absorption.'

'All right, I get the point.'

'Then why are you taking them?' Again, Janine lapsed into silence. 'I think,' Ollie said carefully, 'you've been using them in a desperate attempt to lose weight.'

'That's rubbish.'

'Is it? Do you remember what you weighed twelve months ago?

Very slowly, Janine replied, 'A hundred and twenty pounds. I remember because it was just before I had to do the audition for the Royal Ballet School.'

'Which means,' Ollie did a quick calculation,

'you've lost thirty pounds in twelve months!'

'That's not much. You hear about people losing more than that all the time. Some women win prizes for slimming – you see them on TV adverts.'

'True,' Ollie admitted, 'but they're people who had serious weight problems.'

'So do I.'

'A hundred and twenty pounds is pretty low for somebody of your height.'

'But I was putting on weight and the audition for the Royal Ballet School was getting closer. As Mum never stopped telling me, I'm sixteen now, and it would probably be my last chance.'

'So you started to diet,' Ollie suggested, 'and you've carried on ever since.'

'I told you, I have to watch my weight. There's nothing wrong with that, lots of people do.'

'Yes,' Ollie admitted, 'I know. I do. But most of us know when to stop. I don't think you do any more.'

'Why can't you leave me alone?'

'Because,' Ollie said steadily, 'I think you're suffering from anorexia nervosa.'

'What's that when it's at home?'

'A condition which often affects people who've overdone their slimming.'

'Well, that's not me.'

Ollie pressed on. 'It's a very serious illness, involving loss of appetite and an aversion to food. It can lead to noticeable thinness, tiredness and in extreme cases, if not treated in time, even death.'

'I've already told you,' Janine insisted, 'I'm not ill. Look, have you finished with my leg? Because if so, I'd like to get out of here.'

The senior staff nurse, who was washing the plaster of her hands, said over her shoulder. 'You'll have to stay where you are for a bit longer while it sets.'

Janine said to Ollie, 'Then I want to see, what was her name, Nurse Heywood?'

'Why?'

'Because when I first got here, she said she was rr y, what do you call it?'

'Named nurse?'

'That's it. She said, if I wasn't happy with my treatment, I should ask to speak to her. Well, I'm not happy and I want to talk to her.'

'Look, Janine,' Ollie pleaded with her, 'I'm only trying to help. We can offer you treatment before you get any worse.'

But Janine ignored her. 'I want you to get Nurse Heywood for me.'

Ollie shrugged her resignation. 'OK, that's your right, I'll go and get her, but—'

'Now, please!' Janine said it so fiercely she almost growled.

8

OLLIE SOUGHT OUT Ba and confessed, 'I've really blown it now. Janine flatly refuses to admit she has a problem and on top of that, she wants to complain to you about the way I've been treating her.'

'Oh dear.'

'The thing is, I know I'm right. She's lost twenty-five per cent of her bodyweight.'

'Where is she now?'

'Seething in the plaster room.'

'Right, I'll go and hear what she has to say,' Ba said.

'She'll probably take more notice of you,' Ollie admitted, while trying hard not to sound disappointed that she'd failed.

'I'm only going as her named nurse,' Ba assured her. 'You've started the rest; it would be pointless for me to take over at this stage.'

'But I don't see what else I can do. She won't listen to me.'

'Nurse Smith,' Ba chided, 'I hope the Health Service hasn't spent a fortune on your training just to have you quit when you meet your first little setback?'

'No, but—'

'Good. Otherwise I might begin to think the money would have been better spent on a decent coffee machine for the staff room.'

'But what else can I do?'

'I think,' Ba said, 'it's high time you brought her parents in on this. Why don't you talk to them?'

'Are you sure?' Ollie looked uncertain. 'If I can't get through to their daughter, how will I ever be able to convince the Connollys, especially her mother?'

'You've got to tell them how to look after Janine's leg and she'll need an appointment at the fracture clinic. Sort those things out with them first and then see where that leads.

Vee was clearing up a recently vacated cubicle when Jill walked past and stopped to ask, 'Did you find out anything more about our new girl?'

'Not much,' Vee answered.

Suspecting Vee had found out far more than she was letting on, Jill continued to press her. 'Come on, you must have found out something.

She owned up about having to leave London, but she didn't say why.'

'We spent most of the time chatting about her schooldays,' Vee said casually.

Jill pulled a face. 'How thrilling.'

'Look, Jill,' Vee said, 'I'd better tell you straight out, rather than let you find out some other way – Ollie's going to be staying at my flat for a while.'

Jill looked upset. 'Oh, so that's how things are!'

'As a matter of fact,' Vee said, 'I quite like Ollie, she's good fun.'

'You soon find out who your real friends are round here!' Jill said huffily and marched off down the corridor so quickly she almost collided with Tarquin.

Although Vee couldn't hear what they said to each other, it was obviously an enjoyable conversation judging by the smile it put back on Jill's face. Not to mention Tarquin's affectionate pat on Jill's shoulder.

'Oh, Jill,' Vee murmured to herself, 'I hope you know what you're getting yourself into!'

Mr and Mrs Connolly listened attentively while Ollie explained how to look after their daughter. 'The main things are, Janine mustn't put any weight on the cast for forty-eight hours until it's completely set. Then, to avoid it crumbling, the plaster must be kept dry at all times. Keep a lookout for any discoloration or signs of pins and needles, which would happen if the cast is too tight. If she's in pain, it's all right for Janine to take pain killers and it would help if, when she rests, she keeps her leg up on something like a stool. This is her appointment card for the Fracture Clinic, but if there are any problems, particularly in the early stages, don't hesitate to come back to Accident and Emergency; don't wait for the clinic appointment.'

Mr Connolly nodded, 'Thank you, Nurse.'

His wife was still looking anxious. 'How long will it take to mend? She's supposed to be joining the Royal Ballet School.'

Ollie sidestepped the question. 'That's very difficult to say. It will be quite a while before she'll be able to take the kind of strain ballet dancing imposes, but the specialist in the Fracture Clinic should be able to give you a clearer idea as to how she's progressing.' Ollie decided to take the plunge. 'But there is one thing which could affect her recovery rate.'

'What's that?' Mrs Connolly asked anxiously.

'Her diet.'

'I always see she gets lots of fresh, healthy food,' vowed Mrs Connolly.

'Janine is seriously underweight.'

Mrs Connolly bridled. 'I hope you're not suggesting I starve my daughter?'

'Not at all,' Ollie said quickly. 'But I think, unknown to you, she's been severely restricting her diet.'

'She is very small-boned.'

'I know,' Ollie agreed, 'but that wouldn't account for the weight loss she's suffered. Have you noticed anything unusual about the way she's been behaving lately?'

Understandably, they both looked very concerned. 'What on earth do you mean?' Mr Connolly asked. 'You're not suggesting she's on drugs, or something?'

'No, of course not. I'm sorry, I'm not putting this very well,' Ollie said. 'Let's take something very specific. Does she pay frequent visits to the bathroom?'

The suggestion obviously hit its mark. Mrs Connolly immediately came back. 'But that's not unusual with teenagers. They spend hours fussing with their hair and faces. I'm sure you do too.'

'Judging by how she looked when she was brought in,' Ollie pointed out, 'Janine wears as little make-up as I do. You see, I'm certain she's been using laxatives as a misguided method of keeping down her weight, and the long-term consequences of that could be very serious.'

'I've never heard such nonsense!' Mrs Connolly scoffed.

'She has a large quantity in her bag and they weren't prescribed by a doctor.'

'She was probably constipated,' Mrs Connolly said. 'I don't think that proves anything.'

But Mr Connolly put a restraining hand on his wife's arm. 'Just a minute, Mary. She does go to the bathroom a lot, and I've noticed how thin she's been getting lately. I wondered if she was worried about something.'

'Well, she may have lost a little weight,' Mrs Connolly said, 'but weight does fluctuate. She'll easily put it back on again.'

'That would depend on the circumstances. Just now, Mr Connolly, you said you wondered if she was worried about something. Has Janine been under a lot of pressure?'

'Dancing is very strenuous,' Mrs Connolly pointed out.

'I wasn't thinking so much of physical pressure as psychological,' Ollie said. 'When I was talking to Janine just now, she said she got very worried about putting on weight just before the Royal Ballet School audition. Maybe she felt that she would be letting you down if she didn't pass.'

'Not letting me down,' Mrs Connolly interjected, 'letting herself down. I mean, that was the moment she'd been working towards for years.'

'You'd been working towards for years,' Mr Connolly said quietly.

His wife turned on him. 'What's that supposed to mean?'

'Come on, Mary,' he said gently, 'you've been on at her about dancing almost from the day she was born.'

'But it was for her, Dan,' Mrs Connolly stressed.

'Was it?'

'Of course it was!'

Her husband looked at her carefully. 'Are you sure ballet isn't what you would have liked to have done yourself, if your family had had the money?'

'Well, yes, of course, but—' her voice trailed away.

'All I'm saying is,' he pressed on, 'we never really asked Janine what she wanted to do, did we?'

Mrs Connolly looked perplexed. 'But she was always so keen.'

'Janine's a very talented artist too, but you never liked her doing that.'

'She couldn't earn a living scribbling, could she?'

'I bet there are as many out-of-work ballet dancers, as there are artists,' Mr Connolly said defensively.

Not wishing to be drawn into their private argument, Ollie said, 'Janine obviously enjoys dancing, Mrs Connolly, but sometimes children try too hard to please their parents.'

'You're surely not suggesting she's been doing it all these years just to please me?'

Ollie tried to avoid answering the question. 'Janine's obviously very talented, otherwise she would never have passed the audition, but if she thought she had to pass the audition, gaining weight at the critical time may have really worried her.'

'But once she'd passed . . .?'

'It isn't that simple,' Ollie explained. 'Once she'd got into a poor eating pattern, it may have been difficult for her to break it and when dieting didn't give her the result she was after, Janine started using the laxatives. What she didn't know was that it's a very hit or miss solution to the problem. When it didn't work she probably just kept increasing the dosage.'

'Poor kid!' Mr Connolly muttered.

'The other thing is,' Ollie said, 'I suspect from something she said that Janine's stopped having periods.'

Mrs Connolly's mouth set firmly. 'I'm sure that isn't true. I'd have known. She'd have told me.'

Ollie pressed on. 'I'm sure she's reached the stage where she's suffering from anorexia nervosa but, although I've talked to Janine, she won't admit to having a problem and, until she does, we can't do very much to help her.'

'I'm not surprised,' Mrs Connolly snapped. 'I think it's an outrageous suggestion. If I make sure she has three good meals a day, she'll soon put back any weight she's lost.'

'You must try to understand,' Ollie pointed out, 'by now Janine's problems are mainly psychological. For a start, anorexics get what's known as a distorted body image. They're so convinced that it's important to be thin, they can look in a mirror but not see how thin they've actually become.'

Mrs Connolly looked quite shocked. 'I wish you'd stop using that terrible word, anorexic. I'm quite sure my daughter's nothing of the kind.'

Ollie pointed out, 'But, if she is, she'll have developed a strong aversion to food and she wouldn't suddenly be able to eat vast quantities. She would probably vomit up anything she ate, which would only make matters worse.'

'So what do we do?' Mr Connolly asked.

'That's the whole point,' Ollie said. 'Janine will need a great deal of professional help, and accepting the need for that is the first, crucial step, but the one which I haven't been able to get her to take. I very much doubt if I will now without your help.'

'Well, you won't get it from me,' Mrs Connolly said scornfully. 'It's a ridiculous idea. Where is Janine?'

'In the plaster room with Senior Staff Nurse Heywood. I'm afraid she's complaining about me,' Ollie revealed. 'Janine thinks I've been bullying her, but all I've been doing is trying to get her to face up to reality.'

'I'm hardly surprised she thinks you've been

badgering her,' Mrs Connolly said, 'if this is the sort of nonsense you've been coming out with. We came to get her leg treated, not to have these wild allegations thrown at us.'

Mr Connolly reproved her. 'Mary! I think that's uncalled for. The nurse is merely giving you her professional opinion.'

'Well, I for one,' Mrs Connolly bridled, 'don't believe a single word of it. It's preposterous.'

'Would you have been any more likely to believe it,' Mr Connolly wondered, 'if Madame from the Dancing Academy had said it?'

Her husband's suggestion clearly threw Mrs Connolly off balance. 'I don't know,' she shrugged, but then hastily denied the implication. 'No, of course I wouldn't.'

Mr Connolly looked unconvinced. 'Look, I think the best thing to do is get Janine in here and discuss it with her. Let's see what she has to say.'

Mrs Connolly look horrified. 'Don't you think she's already suffered enough today?'

'What I think is,' Mr Connolly said, very firmly, 'Nurse Smith has told us something very serious about our daughter's health and, as responsible parents, we have a duty to investigate that thoroughly before it's too late.'

Ollie could have hugged Mr Connolly for his show of support, though Mrs Connolly's expression of angry disbelief wasn't too encouraging.

Jill was finishing a cheese roll in the staff restaurant when Angus McFee stopped beside her. 'Well spotted, Nurse Thomson.'

Jill looked puzzled. 'I'm sorry, I don't understand.'

Angus laughed. 'I mean, you were quite write about Sarah's cats. I must say, it really helps us doctors when nurses pick up on that sort of conversation with patients. The results of her blood test have come back. She's got toxoplasmosis. The results show antibodies are present in her bloodstream.

'A raised IgG?' Jill asked anxiously.

Angus looked impressed. 'My word, we have done our homework! No, fortunately for the baby's sake, IgM. But she's not out of the woods yet. The lab will need more blood for a culture before we tell her anything.'

9

As Ba and Ollie took Janine back to her cubicle, Ollie couldn't help wondering if Ba might still exercise her seniority and take over the conversation, but although she stayed, Ba showed no inclination to speak.

It was Janine who immediately said to her parents, 'My leg's done, I'm tired and I'd like to go home now.'

Ollie opened her mouth to reply, but was beaten by Mr Connolly. 'In a minute, Janine, but first there's this other matter to discuss.'

'What other matter?' Janine asked rudely.

'Nurse Smith says you've been dieting so severely that you're very underweight,' her father replied.

'That's not true!' Janine snapped.

'And that you've been taking laxatives.'

Janine turned on Ollie and hissed, 'You had no right to tell them!'

'I'm sorry,' Ollie apologised, 'but you didn't leave me any choice.'

'Traitor!'

Her father stirred uncomfortably in his chair. 'Janine, Nurse Smith has only acted in your best interests and your mother and I feel very grateful to her for telling us.'

'Except that it's all lies,' Janine blurted out. 'There's nothing wrong with me, apart from my leg. She's made it all up and I wish you'd all leave me alone.'

Mrs Connolly stroked Janine's arm. 'That's what I said, dear.'

'But if it were true,' her father continued, calmly, 'and you carry on the way you are, don't you realise you could make yourself seriously ill and even die?'

'That's rubbish,' Janine said obstinately. 'I'm looking after my weight, just as I always have, so that I can do ballet. That is what you want, isn't it?'

'Yes, of course,' her mother admitted, 'but I wouldn't want you to do anything silly.'

'I'm not.'

Mr Connolly patted his daughter's hand. 'The trouble with seeing someone every day is you tend not to see what's right under your nose. Until now, I thought you were a bit thin but I hadn't noticed just how thin.'

Janine snatched her hand away. 'I'm not

thin. Just look at me, I'm positively gross!'

Her father looked upset by the blank wall of resistance his daughter was putting up. 'Darling, that's simply not true!' he said. 'I don't understand why a healthy, active girl like you needs to diet at all.'

'If you don't understand that, you don't understand anything,' Janine murmured.

'Then perhaps you would explain to me,' Mr Connolly suggested.

Ollie watched and waited, knowing that the subject was poised on a knife edge and Janine might go either way. She could open up or she might say nothing at all. Ollie held her breath.

'All my life,' Janine began slowly, 'Mum's been going on at me about what I eat.'

Her mother took immediate offence. 'That's simply not true!'

Ollie physically flinched at Mrs Connolly's interruption. But, to her enormous relief, Janine came back strongly.

'Isn't it? I remember, I must have been about five or six at the time, coming out of a tap class we'd gone to straight from school and telling you I was starving. I begged you to buy me some chocolate on the way home, but you said I couldn't have any because it would make me fat.'

'I don't remember that particular occasion,' Mrs Connolly admitted, 'but in any case, that was ages ago and probably an isolated incident. You're blowing it up out of proportion.'

'It might not have meant much to you, but it did to me and it was always the same!' Janine wailed. 'Everything I did was affected by my dancing. I used to miss birthday parties I'd been invited to, and once I wasn't allowed to go with the school trip to a pantomime, just because it clashed with a class.'

'But I thought you loved dancing,' Mrs Connolly protested, 'and anyway, you always hated going to school.'

'The reason I hated going to school,' Janine declared passionately, 'was because they all thought I was a weirdo. They were all allowed to do things I wasn't because of my dancing and so they decided I was stuck up.'

For the first time Mrs Connolly looked crestfallen. 'You should have said.'

'I did!' Janine said quietly. 'All the time, but you just didn't hear me. You only thought of one thing and that was dancing. As far as you were concerned, nothing else mattered. Remember last February, when I got my very first proper valentine card? I was absolutely thrilled silly, but what did you say, Mother?'

'I don't remember,' Mrs Connolly murmured.

'I do. You said, "you mustn't fill your head with a lot of nonsense like that, there'll be plenty of time for boyfriends when you're a prima ballerina." But how do you think I felt, when there were girls in my school with steady boyfriends and I've never so much as been to a disco, or a cinema, with a boy? Do you know, I'm the only girl at the Dance Academy without a boyfriend?'

'You were also the only girl in the Academy to pass an audition for the Royal Ballet School,' Mrs Connolly said emphatically.

'But the other mothers don't see any harm in their daughters having boyfriends.'

'But that's probably why their daughters didn't pass and you did,' Mrs Connolly said smugly. 'To be a top-class dancer requires total dedication.'

'Dancing's become an obsession with you, Mum.'

'This is all very well,' Mrs Connolly said curtly, 'but I don't see what it has to do with your dieting to the point of making yourself ill.'

Janine looked steadily at her mother for a

moment before she said, 'When you got the date for the interview and audition at the Royal Ballet School, you practically went into orbit! From then on, there was nothing else in our lives. Day and night, we talked of nothing else. We ate, drank and slept that one subject.'

'That's true,' Mr Connolly agreed.

'It's hardly surprising,' his wife said indignantly. 'That day was the culmination of all those years of work. Hours of barre practice, appearing in shows and taking exams. It really was the chance of a lifetime.'

'Oh, you left me in no doubt about that,' Janine said bitterly. 'This was the moment you'd been waiting for all your life and didn't I know it! I was made to feel that, if I failed the audition, I'd be throwing away all you'd ever done for me. All those sacrifices you'd made for me and not just the hours of taking me everywhere, but the money too. All the things we'd gone without because the money had all been spent on my training and the things I needed like new point shoes or leotards, when what we all needed was a holiday. I remember you being desperate for some new shoes, but my ballet shoes got reblocked instead.'

'We thought your future was far more

important than me getting new clothes, didn't we, Dan?'

'True,' he agreed.

Janine's smile showed genuine gratitude, though it soon faded. 'Which is very kind of you both, but just look at that suit Dad's wearing. It's so old and baggy! Sometimes I think he must have been wearing it all my life! And that was the suit I used to see every night during the weeks before the audition, until it became a sort of symbol. If I failed the audition, I'd be wasting all those years you'd suffered having to wear that awful suit. He needs new frames for his glasses, but instead he sticks them together with tape. If I didn't pass I'd be throwing back in your faces all the years of scrimping and saving you'd done for me, and saying you'd done it all for nothing.' Janine shook her head as she remembered how she'd felt at the time. 'I knew I couldn't let you down. I had to pass that audition at all costs. And at the same time, there I was, looking at the other dancers in the Academy, who were all incredibly slim and supple, and I was convinced I wasn't going to make it. I knew I was going to fail and you'd both be so disappointed in me, particularly you, Mum.'

Mrs Connolly, whose eyes had filled with

tears as she listened to her daughter, said, 'Oh, Janine!'

'So I tried to lose some weight,' Janine went on, 'but you kept feeding me up to give me more energy, until I began to feel like a calf being fattened for slaughter. I got so desperate I started using the laxatives.'

'And you're still using them now, aren't you?' Ollie asked. Seconds ticked away as they waited for Janine to acknowledge this basic truth.

Janine looked down at her hands which were twisting together in her lap. Then one hand strayed towards the top of her plaster cast and she plucked nervously at the edge of the padding with a fingernail. The silence went on and on before she eventually said, in a voice barely above a whisper, 'Yes!'

Ollie sighed with relief, but Mrs Connolly's reaction was quite different. 'What you're saying,' she was grim-faced and forcing the words out, 'is that I drove you to take them. I've brought you to this state.'

But Mr Connolly calmly intervened. 'Mary, I don't think there's anything to be gained by blaming anyone. The most important thing is, how do we solve the problem?'

Ollie looked at Ba, but she merely indicated that Ollie should go ahead. 'Janine, it's very brave of you to own up to having a problem. The first practical step is to get you to see the on-call psychiatrist.'

Mrs Connolly looked shocked. 'A psychiatrist?'

'Your daughter is going to need a lot of support to come to terms with everything,' Ollie explained, 'and, although your help is crucial, she'll need a lot of professional advice too.'

'And I suppose,' Mrs Connolly added quietly, 'this means the end of all ambition to be a top ballerina?'

Janine touched her mother for the first time, laying a hand gently on hers. 'Not necessarily. In fact, I don't know what it means yet. Because you are right, I do love dancing.'

'But just not as much as me,' her mother said.

'Whatever happens, I'll always dance,' Janine assured her, 'even if I only end up doing shows with the local amateurs.'

Mrs Connolly visibly brightened. 'Aren't they doing West Side Story this year? There's lots of dancing in that.' She stopped and laughed at herself. 'There I go again! Trying to make plans for you. But, to be honest, Janine, I would far rather you never danced again, if this is what it does to you.' She was looking, as if for the first time, at Janine's incredibly thin arm and wrist. Gently, Mrs Connolly raised her daughter's hand and held it to her cheek. The tears, which Mrs Connolly had managed to hold back until that moment, suddenly poured out, streaming down her face.

'Mum, don't!' Janine murmured. 'While my leg's getting better, we'll have plenty of time to talk about what I'm going to do and maybe Dad could help me with my drawing.'

'I'd love to,' he said.

Mrs Connolly wiped her tears away with a crumpled tissue. 'You two and your scribbling,' she said, but without any of her usual sharpness.

'We'll go and sort out the psychiatrist for you,' Ollie said, and they left the family together.

Ollie and Ba had only gone a few steps down the corridor when Ollie turned and said, 'I feel as if I've just gone twelve rounds in the ring with Sylvester Stallone!'

'Oh, I've done that!' Ba said scathingly. 'It was a piece of cake compared to one shift in A and E! Anyway, it was probably easy, compared to breaking the news to Tarquin that he's over-looked an anorexic.'

Angus and Jill went into Sarah's cubicle, Angus clutching the case notes. 'Sarah, we've got the results of your tests now.'

'There's something wrong. I can tell by your faces,' Sarah said anxiously. 'Is it the baby? Am I going to lose the baby?' She grabbed the doctor's hand.

'No, I think not,' Angus patted Sarah's hand and gave her a quiet smile, 'but you've had a very narrow escape.'

'Please, tell me what's wrong.'

'You're suffering from toxoplasmosis.'

'What's that?'

'It's an infection which is very common in humans,' Angus explained. 'Many of us have it without really noticing. Anyone who eats pork or lamb can get it and usually it's not very seri-ous. Our immune system can cope. But, with your being pregnant, that raises rather different problems.'

'Not the baby!' Sarah pleaded, hugging her stomach.

'I think, in your case, the baby's going to be

fine,' Angus reassured her. 'You'll need to have further tests done, first of all to establish how long you've had the infection and then to see if the baby's actually caught it.'

Sarah asked, 'How can you tell?'

'More tests and scans.'

'And if the baby has got it?'

'Because it's developed during the third trimester of your pregnancy there's no risk of miscarriage or stillbirth and it's much less serious for the baby. Had you caught it earlier, there could have been all kinds of complications, but as it is, even if the baby is infected, there are treatments and I think antimalarial drugs should clear it up with no harm done.'

'Oh, what a relief!' Sarah sighed.

'We'll need to keep you in for observation for a few days, but that's all. OK?'

'Thank you, Doctor.'

'You should thank Nurse Thomas too,' Angus pointed out. 'She was the one who spotted the source of your infection. The last case of toxoplasmosis I saw was in the Highlands, when a shepherd's wife caught it from the sheep.'

'I was wondering about that,' Sarah said, 'because I don't eat meat, I'm a vegetarian.'

'But you did tell me you keep cats,' Jill explained, 'and they can easily pass the infection on to humans from the meats they eat. Perhaps, because you're pregnant and your husband's away and can't help, you haven't been emptying their litter tray often enough. It would only need you to handle one of the cats and not wash your hands properly, for you to pick up the infection.'

Sarah's mouth dropped open in astonishment. 'You mean I've been putting our baby's life at risk, all because I've been taking in a few strays?'

'There shouldn't be a problem this time,' said Angus, 'but I'd make sure any other cats you decide to give a home to get checked by a vet first.'

Dr Yasmin Patel, one of the unit's registrars who was coming on duty for the next shift, was chatting with Tarquin. 'Been busy?' she asked him.

'Fairly. Usual crop of burns and scratches. I lost a drunken diabetic in a coma last night and we had two Dead on Arrivals from a motorcycle accident. I hate DOAs – so much paperwork for absolutely no return. Then we had an RTA around midday today, one with a severe cranial injury who's still up in theatre.' He paused, looking thoughtful. 'At least I think that was today. Time just flies when you're having fun.'

'I know the feeling,' she said with a brief smile. Looking at the status board, she observed, 'Is the sprained wrist still here?'

'Oh, no, he's gone,' Tarquin said. 'Where's the duster disappeared to this time?'

'It's here, on the floor,' she said, handing it to him so that he could wipe the entry off the board. 'That girl with the broken tibia's been in a long time. Why the delay?'

'There was a hold-up with X-ray while we were sorting the RTA, but I thought she'd gone.'

'Thought, Doctor Royston?' Dr Patel asked coolly. 'I hope this isn't another patient you've mislaid, like the old lady we eventually found under the bed last week.'

Tarquin winced. She was obviously never going to let him forget that one. 'That was Nurse Thomson's fault. She was supposed to have been applying a dressing.'

'Nurse Thomson was in Crash at the time, Doctor Royston, so I hardly think it could have been her fault.'

'Well, maybe it was Ba.'

'And maybe it wasn't,' Dr Patel suggested. Her right eyebrow rose critically on her broad, high forehead. 'You're so quick to grab any praise that's going, and too ready to shift blame on to others.'

Yasmin's career had involved a difficult struggle to overcome all kinds of prejudice. Not only racist but sexist too. Having qualified and achieved her position as registrar at Whiston City General, she wasn't going to let herself be undermined by the likes of Tarquin Royston. Given the slightest chance, he would be only too willing to stab her in the back in his fight to reach the top. Yasmin always felt it was wise to let Tarquin know she was watching his every move.

In reception, a singing drunk, who'd wandered in off the street was serenading Maureen at the top of his voice.

'Please, you must be quiet!' Maureen said, raising her voice. 'This is a hospital.'

The drunken man carried on singing. Between verses, he took swigs from a bottle of foul-smelling liquid. He had also brought a milk bottle containing some muddy water and a single, rather crumpled red rose, which he placed on the desk in front of Maureen.

He'd been leaning heavily on the desk but, with each swig, he sank lower and lower. Strangely, the lower he sank, the louder his voice became.

'Stop it this minute,' Maureen said crossly, 'or I shall have to call security.'

The drunk paused, his face by now level with the desk which he gripped as if it were the side of a lifeboat he was desperately trying to board. Then he took a long gulp from his bottle, opened his mouth to sing and slumped silently to the floor.

At that instant the self-important, plump figure of Norman Eames, the general manager of A and E, bustled into reception. He was accompanied by a tall, distinguished looking man with a neatly trimmed beard.

Stepping over the drunk, who had begun to snore, Norman Eames introduced his guest to Maureen. 'This is Sir Richard Askins, a member of our board of management. Maureen Imison, one of our longest-serving receptionists.'

Sir Richard nodded.

'Getting on all right with the computer now, Maureen?' Norman asked, though his mind was clearly elsewhere.

'Yes, thank you.'

'Maureen sometimes has difficulty interfacing with the latest technology,' he explained to Sir Richard.

But Sir Richard was rather more interested in the man lying at his feet. 'Miss Imison, did you know you have a patient lying on the floor?'

'Well, at least he can't fall any farther,' Maureen said, without thinking.

Sir Richard wasn't sure he'd heard properly. 'I beg your pardon?'

'I was just about to deal with him,' Maureen said, reaching for the phone and dialling.

Sir Richard turned to Norman Eames. 'Time's getting on. Shall we go?'

'Oh, yes,' Eames said, almost bowing as he indicated the way through to the unit. But he found time to dodge back and say confidentially to Maureen, 'I think the flower is a nice touch, as long as it doesn't come off the budget, but do try and find a proper vase.'

'Idiot!' Maureen muttered at his retreating figure and then, when her call was answered, she said into the phone, 'Sister Broadhurst? Could you please send Dean out here? I've got Secondhand Rose asleep on the floor again and by the way, little Norman's waddled through with someone. I think he said Sir Richard something-or-other. Yes, Askins, that was it.'

As Ba completed her paperwork, Ollie heaved a huge sigh. 'I feel as though I've spent the whole day on one patient.'

'You get days like that,' Ba agreed, 'and then others when you see so many people, at the end of the shift you can't picture any of them.'

Tarquin appeared round the corner. 'Why is that broken tibia still here? I thought we'd finished with her ages ago.'

'Doctor Royston, I was just coming to see you about that young girl,' Ba said. 'Nurse Smith noticed she was very thin, and—'

'Not very thin,' Tarquin interrupted. 'She's a gymnast or something, isn't she?

'A ballet dancer, and she's approximately thirty pounds underweight,' Ba said coolly.

Tarquin nodded. 'Oh, I see.'

'After a good deal of conversation with the girl, Nurse Smith has got her to admit she's anorexic.'

'Oh, the old slimmer's disease,' Tarquin said dismissively. 'Very trendy.'

'But it will affect the girl's recovery rate,' Ba

added rather heavily. 'It might not look very good for you, Doctor Royston, if it's missing from her notes when the girl reports to the fracture clinic.'

Unabashed, Tarquin asked, 'True. Well, I'd better enter it up now, hadn't I, Staff?'

'Yes, Doctor, and shall we ring the on-call psychiatrist and ask someone to talk to her before she leaves?'

'What?' Tarquin half laughed and then changed his mind. 'I suppose so.' Turning on Ollie, he added fiercely, 'And next time you come up with a bright idea, Nurse Smith, I'd be grateful if you'd let me know first. After all, we are supposed to be a team.'

'Idiot!' Ollie muttered under her breath at his departing figure. 'I mean, you save his skin and the man still isn't grateful.'

The words had hardly left her lips, when Margery Broadhurst's voice boomed out from the far end of the unit. 'Nurse Smith, come here at once please!'

'Oh, no, what now?'

Ba clapped her hand to her mouth. 'I forgot to warn you.'

Ollie looked worried. 'Warn me – about what?'

'That a selection of Suits are coming down from admin. One of them insisted on seeing you before the end of the shift.'

'Oh, no!' Ollie groaned. 'Just when I thought I'd got something right for a change. What can I possibly have done wrong now?'

10

AS OLLIE SAW a serious-looking Margery Broadhurst coming down the aisle between the cubicles to meet her, she knew exactly how the French aristocrats must have felt as they walked towards the guillotine.

'I have no idea what all this fuss is about, Nurse Smith,' Sister Broadhurst said, her voice heavy with disapproval, 'but please, in front of management, watch what you say. And could you please sort out your hair!'

'Yes, Sister,' Ollie said. '

Word that the Suits were on the Unit had got around and quite a group had found excuses to do things close by. Amongst them was Jill Thomson, who'd heard a whisper that her rival was in some kind of trouble, something she didn't want to miss.

As Ollie arrived in front of the two visitors, Margery hastily performed the formal introductions. 'Nurse Smith, this is Norman Eames, the A and E general manager, and this gentleman is a member of the hospital's board, Sir Richard Askins.'

Ollie smiled. 'Hello, Dickie.'

'Nurse Smith!' Margery was outraged. All her worst fears about this girl were now fully justified. She spluttered, 'We should at least do people the courtesy of using their titles.'

'Sorry,' Ollie said casually. 'Hello, Uncle Dickie.'

The distinguished gentleman's face broke into a smile. 'Hello, Ollie. Good to see you again.'

Mouths dropped open around them, as the two hugged.

Margery stammered, 'I'm sorry, I hadn't realised you two were related.'

'We aren't,' Sir Richard said. 'But I'm a very old friend of the family.'

On hearing that Ollie's family had friends on the board, Jill Thomson wasn't the only one thinking it was hardly surprising Ollie had been able to get a job at Whiston City General.

Unaware of the filthy look Jill was giving her, Ollie explained, 'Uncle Dickie spent ages trying to teach me how to keep a straight bat at cricket when I was about six.'

Norman Eames, who had been feeling rather

left out, said with hearty enthusiasm, 'Always useful.'

This pointless remark earned him a withering look from Sir Richard, who continued, 'Ollie, although it's always a pleasure to see you, I particularly wanted to get down tonight, not just to welcome you and wish you luck in your new job, but because I received a phone call about you this morning.'

'Oh, really?'

'It was from a very old friend of mine, Josh Giffins.'

Ollie looked puzzled. 'I don't think I know him.'

'Possibly not, but this morning you came across his daughter, Liz.'

Light came into Ollie's eyes. 'Oh, yes, but I didn't know who she was.'

Sister Broadhurst, who was getting rather irritated with her unit being disturbed for nothing more than the exchange of social chit-chat, said, 'Well, if you'll forgive us, it's coming to the end of the shift and we've still got a lot to do.'

'Yes, of course,' Sir Richard agreed. 'I'll only keep you a moment longer. I felt I should officially pass on Josh's thanks to Ollie for helping his daughter. Liz was out riding this morning, and her horse threw her. She suffered a very nasty fall and she was extremely lucky Ollie happened to be passing on her way here. Ollie stopped Liz's riding companions from moving her off the road, and she stayed with her until the ambulance arrived.'

Ollie blushed. 'Anyone would have done the same.'

'But they didn't, Ollie,' Sir Richard said, 'and you prevented a bad accident being made infinitely worse. Liz suffered a serious spine injury and may well have ended up paralysed if she had been moved before the ambulance arrived. So, well done. Now, must go. Sorry to delay you, Sister Broadhurst. Love to your folks, Ollie.'

'Thanks, Dickie.'

Sir Richard left with Norman Eames still fluttering round his ankles like an overexcited spaniel.

Sister Broadhurst was the first to speak to Ollie. 'So, that was why you were late this morning? You really should have said. Well done.'

Jill Thomson murmured to Vee, 'A big fuss about nothing, if you ask me.'

Vee laughed at her. 'Oooh! Pull your claws

back in, Jill, before you scratch us all!'

But Jill wasn't amused. 'Pity we haven't all got daddies with rich, influential friends who can get us jobs.'

But Vee was no longer listening. She'd gone up to clap Ollie on the back. 'Good for you. Have twenty brownie points.'

'Thanks.'

'Look, it's nearly time to go,' Vee pointed out. 'I was wondering about that massive trunk of yours.'

'You make me sound like an elephant.'

'I just wondered if I ought to phone for a cab to pick us up in about twenty minutes, when we've changed?'

'That would be great,' Ollie agreed. 'I just want to say goodbye and good luck to Janine first.'

'Oh, she's already gone,' Vee said. 'The psychiatric registrar came down for a chat and then I saw Dean helping Janine and her parents out into reception.'

Ollie looked upset. 'I thought she might at least have said goodbye. Maybe she hasn't forgiven me for giving the game away to her parents.'

'That's the way nursing in A and E works,' Ba

said quietly. 'One minute it's, "Nurse! Nurse! Stop it bleeding, stop it hurting," and they want your total attention, the next minute they're patched up and gone.'

'Who's gone?' asked Sister Broadhurst, breaking off her conversation with Dr Patel.

'Janine,' Ba replied.

'Yes, bit of a delay with that one,' Tarquin said importantly, 'after I discovered she was anorexic.'

Margery Broadhurst fixed him with a look and said, 'I think that was down to Nurse Smith, Doctor Royston.'

Dr Patel smiled and shook her head, pleased that Tarquin hadn't got away with that one.

'Yes, well, whatever,' Tarquin said, turning away, 'at least she's another one we can wipe off the board. Where's the wretched duster gone this time?'

'Oh, here you are,' Ollie suggested, helpfully handing him a scrap of cloth. 'Use this.'

Tarquin wiped Janine's name off the board and was surprised when everyone burst out laughing. It was only then that he noticed he was cleaning the board with Ollie's pants. 'I suppose you think that's funny?' he snapped, hurling them into the trash can and stomping off down the corridor, snatching his white coat off so violently he ripped the pocket.

Ollie said to Vee, 'I think we'd better get out of here while the going's good!' As Ollie walked past Ba, she said, 'I hope Simon's going to be OK.'

'Thanks, I'm sure he will be,' Bee said, glancing at her watch. 'Heavens, I ought to go and pick him up in a minute.'

'Hope you get some sleep tonight.'

'I will.'

'And, Ba, thanks for everything today.'

'Nurse Smith,' Sister Broadhurst said, as Ollie was about to leave. 'Don't be late tomorrow for our chat and please sort out your hair!'

'I will,' Ollie assured her.

'Have you found somewhere to stay?'

'Vee's putting me up for the time being.'

'All right, off you go then,' Sister Broadhurst said with a brief nod. She watched Ollie walking off towards the staff room to change and turned back to Ba. 'I really don't know what to make of that girl.'

'She's definitely very persistent,' Ba replied. 'It took a good deal to get Janine to admit she actually had a problem.'

'Oh, she's got the gift of the gab all right,'

Margery admitted, 'and she knows all the right people, but on today's showing, I'm still not convinced Nurse Smith takes nursing seriously enough. All that larking about and embarrassing young Doctor Royston.'

'He does ask for it.'

'It's all very well rescuing maidens in distress,' Margery continued, 'but you know, most of our days are made up of sheer gruelling repetition and, unlike Jill, who just gets on with things, I'm not certain that young lady will have the stamina and application to stick it out. I can just see her giving up nursing the moment she's snapped up some rich, eligible doctor.'

'Wouldn't we all?' Ba said.

'Well, I wouldn't for one,' Margery said, 'and you didn't when you had the chance.'

'True! Which reminds me, I'm going to be late for Simon! By the way, how's your mother these days?'

Margery's face creased into a frown. 'I suppose, for eighty-three she's doing quite well, but these last few months she's been behaving oddly. I think it's spending too much time on her own that does it. I can't help wondering if I shall have to put her in a home soon, though it's the last thing I want to do.'

'Looking after her, running a home and holding down a demanding job is a big responsibility.' Ba glanced anxiously at her watch. 'You must excuse me, Margery, I must pick up Simon.'

Vee found a sack trolley for Ollie's cabin trunk and they piled some of the carrier bags on top. They were wheeling it through reception when Maureen called out, 'Ollie! I've got—'

Ollie interrupted her. 'Not more messages?'

'No, someone left this for you.'

Ollie took the large sheet of paper and her face broke into a broad smile when she realised it was the picture Janine had drawn of her. Across one corner Janine had signed it and then written underneath, Thanks for everything. Maybe I could drop by one day and see you.

'I suppose this was her way of saying goodbye,' Ollie said with a pleased grin.

'That's a really good picture of you,' Vee said, looking over Ollie's shoulder, and then added, in a wickedly accurate imitation of Margery Broadhurst, 'especially that terrible hair!'

'What on earth have you got in that trunk?' Maureen asked.

Vee said casually, 'Just one of the patients who didn't make it.'

'He requested burial at sea, hence the cabin trunk,' Ollie added.

Neither of them realised a new patient had come up quietly behind them. When Vee and Ollie turned and caught sight of the woman's horrified expression, they were overcome by a fit of giggles and rapidly wheeled their load towards the exit door.

'Doctor Royston! Doctor Royston!' Jill called out, as she ran down the car park after him.

'What?' he snapped, but when he turned and saw who was following him, his angry face broke into a smile. 'Oh, hello, Nurse Thomson. I'm afraid I'd forgotten about our little arrangement.'

'I'm not surprised,' Jill sympathised, 'with all that silly nonsense going on back there.'

'Some people,' Tarquin said loftily, 'don't seem to realise a hospital isn't a place to be taken lightly. They can be very juvenile.'

'I quite agree,' Jill said, gratefully bathing in the warm glow of Tarquin's appreciation. 'You said I could have a look at your notes.'

'Absolutely,' Tarquin agreed. 'My car's over here.'

They walked together down the dimly lit car

park and Jill watched as he unlocked the passenger door to get to his briefcase. But when he stood up, Tarquin was empty-handed. 'It's just occurred to me,' he said, 'that we could discuss my notes over a Chinese meal?'

Jill was surprised to be asked by someone in Tarquin's position, but although she longed to say yes, she couldn't help wondering about maintaining their professional relationship. 'I don't know.'

'No,' Tarquin said quickly, 'I'm sure you've got other things planned.'

Jill thought of her drab digs and the kind of tasteless food her landlady, Mrs Wrigley, served up with endless tales about the shortcomings of the late Mr Wrigley. 'No,' she said, flattered by Tarquin's invitation, 'I'm not doing anything special.'

'Good!' Tarquin beamed. 'Much more enjoyable to discuss spontaneous pneumothorax over some deep-fried crispy seaweed than out here in the semi darkness.'

'But I'm not really dressed to go anywhere special,' Jill said, looking into Tarquin's eyes.

'My dear Jill,' he said, 'you always look attractive to me, whatever you wear and the place I'm thinking of serves wonderful food, has an excellent-wine list and very discreet lighting. So, I promise, you won't feel the least bit uncomfortable.'

'Busy day, Maureen?' Rob asked, as he came to take over the shift on reception.

'Not too bad,' Maureen said, wheeling her chair out from behind the desk and skilfully negotiating the route past her colleague. 'Apart from that new computer programme.'

Rob nodded sympathetically. 'I'm sure they haven't chased all the bugs out of it yet.'

'That aside,' Maureen laughed, 'I think the biggest job was taking messages for our new nurse, Ollie Smith. If it goes on like today, I think we might need an extra line on the switchboard, just to deal with her distraught boyfriends.'

Ollie and Vee had managed to heave the trunk into the black cab's luggage compartment and had fallen into the back seat. As soon as the taxi set off Ollie wrenched the pins from her hair and shook it free, so that it cascaded down over her shoulders. 'Wow, that feels better!'

They were halfway down the drive, when Vee suddenly pointed out of the window. 'Hey, look who's getting into Tarquin's car! Nurse Jill Thomson, would you believe?'

Ollie frowned. 'Talk about the spider and the fly!'

'I only hope that kid knows what she's doing,' Vee said. 'You don't mess with Tarquin Royston unless you're in the big girls' league.'

'Or,' Ollie suggested, 'you're a big girl's blouse!'

'To go with those pants!' Vee shrieked with delight and, to the bewilderment of the driver, they both collapsed into fits of laughter which lasted until they reached Vee's flat.

Although it had been extensively cleaned and modernised, the building remained a huge Victorian dockside warehouse and, lit only by the streetlights, looked quite gloomy and menacing.

As the taxi drove off, Ollie couldn't help wondering if she'd made the right decision. It was easy to see why Vee was anxious for company down here. These certainly weren't streets she'd enjoy walking through alone on the way to night shift.

But at least it had a lift used to hauling heavy loads, which meant they had no difficulty in getting Ollie's trunk up to the fourth floor where Vee lived.

When Vee unlocked the front door Ollie was pleasantly surprised by what she saw. The flat had been built into one end of the warehouse. Half of it was very high-ceilinged but, at the far end, a wrought-iron staircase led up to a landing, off which opened four doors. Under these bedrooms was a huge cooking and dining area.

Down one whole side there were large double-glazed windows. A sliding door opened on to a narrow balcony which had garden furniture and plants in tubs on it. It looked out across the water of the dock, now a marina. Rows of smart yachts and motor cruisers bobbed up and down in the dark water, that sparkled with the lights spilling out from the other flats.

The furniture was sparse but chunky, and either hi-tech metal and plastic or stripped pine. It might have looked rather cold but for the warm colours of the exposed brick walls, the ethnic print fabrics of the curtains, cushions and upholstery and the large rugs which lay on vast expanses of honey-coloured pine floor.

'Vee! It's absolutely marvellous. How can

you possibly afford—' Ollie broke off. 'Sorry, that was terribly rude of me.'

'You were going to ask, how can I afford this on a health care assistant's pay? Well, let's just say, the guy who sold it had gone broke, so I got it fully furnished as a bargain. Right,' Vee said, changing the subject. 'I am knackered and I want a shower. Shall we order pizzas?'

Although Ollie was mystified as to why Vee had changed the subject so abruptly, she didn't press it. 'I could cook something,' she suggested.

Much as Vee enjoyed Ollie's company, she struck her as being rather posh. Vee imagined Ollie's parents probably had a cook and so it was hardly likely she'd be much good at cooking.

'There's bread and some tins in the cupboard over the sink, but if you open that fridge,' Vee said doubtfully, 'the only things you'll find is a pint of milk, half-a-dozen eggs, some cream, a piece of mouldy cheese and the light staring back at you.'

'Why don't you go and have your shower while I see what I can do?'

Vee, dreading having to survive on a diet of baked beans or poached eggs on toast, reluc-

tantly did as she was told. But, half-an-hour
later, when she emerged, wearing a deep purple
bathrobe, her hair turbaned in a matching
towel, her nostrils were greeted by an astonish-
ing array of appetising smells.

Moreover, the table had been properly laid
and there was even a bottle of wine nestling in
a saucepan, which Ollie had packed with ice.

Vee was amazed. This was streets ahead of
curling up in front of the telly with a pizza,
which was what she usually did after work.
'Where did all this come from?'

'From the cooker', said Ollie, who was ani-
matedly stirring something with a wooden
spoon and had a blob of béchamel sauce on
the end of her nose. 'Vee, you surely don't
imagine the weight of my trunk was solely
due to clothes, do you? You forget I'm used to
ending up in boarding schools where the
food's so awful you can be thinner than Janine
in a week! Nowadays, I never go anywhere
without adequate supplies of food and drink.'

'But you can cook too!' Vee cried in astonishment.

'A cordon bleu cookery course,' said Ollie,
'was the only useful thing I learned in finishing
school.'

'That and the phone numbers of the entire French rugby team.'

'True,' she grinned. 'Hey, this food's nearly ready. Would you open the wine?'

Vee poured two glasses and handed one to Ollie. 'Cheers!'

'Santé!' Ollie said, kicking off her shoes and stretching her tired feet. She took a sip of wine and then sighed contentedly. 'You know, Vee, I think I'm going to enjoy being at Whiston City General.'

CAUSE FOR CONCERN FACT SHEET
ANOREXIA

Research has shown that about 2% of young women are known to suffer from an eating disorder. Many find it very difficult, even frightening, to acknowledge that they are ill, and will often deny the problem even when it is obvious to all around them.

Anorexia is a very complex illness. It is not a 'slimmer's disease', but an expression of deep psychological turmoil. The causes are different for each sufferer, and each individual needs different treatment. Recovery is a long, hard process, but the earlier the illness is recognised and treated, the better the long-term prognosis.

If you need help, or are concerned about a friend or member of your family, you can talk in confidence to someone who understands the problems of anorexia and bulimia:

Eating Disorders Association
TELEPHONE HELPLINE
01603-621414
9am–6.30pm Mon–Fri

YOUTH HELPLINE
(18 yrs and under)
01603-765050
4pm–6pm Mon, Tues & Wed
The Youth Helpline is for young people only. The counsellor will ring back to save the cost of a telephone call.

RECORDED MESSAGE
0891-615466
Calls cost 39p per minute cheap rate
49p per minute other times

If you would like more information about eating disorders, send a stamped addressed envelope to:

Eating Disorders Association
Sackville Place
44 Magdalen Street
Norwich
Norfolk NR3 1JU

The EDA does not offer treatment, but encourages all forms of self help, and can advise on treatment available throughout the UK and give details of the nearest self help group.